ROCKIT CREW

ROCKIT CREW

THE ADVENTURES OF TEENAGE HIP-HOP MISFITS

SHANE ROBITAILLE

ROCKIT CREW
THE ADVENTURES OF TEENAGE
HIP-HOP MISFITS

iUniverse books may be ordered through booksellers or by contacting:

iUniverse
1663 Liberty Drive
Bloomington, IN 47403
www.iuniverse.com
1-800-Authors (1-800-288-4677)

Because of the dynamic nature of the Internet, any web addresses or links contained in this book may have changed since publication and may no longer be valid. The views expressed in this work are solely those of the author and do not necessarily reflect the views of the publisher, and the publisher hereby disclaims any responsibility for them.

Any people depicted in stock imagery provided by Getty Images are models, and such images are being used for illustrative purposes only. Certain stock imagery © Getty Images.

ISBN: 978-1-5320-9465-1 (sc)
ISBN: 978-1-5320-9466-8 (e)

Library of Congress Control Number: 2020902313

Print information available on the last page.

iUniverse rev. date: 11/19/2020

For best friends everywhere and for those
who are brave enough to be different.

PREFACE

THIS IS NOT A STORY about the history of hip-hop; rather it's about four best friends who discovered hip-hop when it was young, the power of friendship in the face of adversity, and how hard it is to be different when the world around you wants you to be like everybody else.

It's not easy being different at any age but it's especially tough for teenagers. I think at some point in our lives, especially when we're young, we need to find out who we are, what we're made of, and take a stand, regardless of what others think. If we don't then we leave it up to the world to do it for us.

In the summer of 1984 four teenage hip-hop misfits dared to be different.

A special thanks to Tam Fricke for her reading, edits and thoughtful suggestions.

And to Sofie Engström von Alten (Instagram @ hyperkitsch) for her totally stellar illustrations.

(ONTENTS

FRIENDS

ALTHOUGH THE VOLUME WAS BLASTED as high as it could go, we could still hear them downstairs. Ms. O'Reilly, the so-called "manager" of the foster home I was living in and her boyfriend were at it again something fierce. The drinking and fighting was in full-force. I was in my bedroom that I shared with three other kids, punching the walls and cranking up the stereo as loud as it would go to drown out the madness. Sometimes punching walls can hurt but it still feels better than doing nothing at all.

As the violence escalated, so did my headache. I couldn't stand the yelling anymore so I tore open the bedroom door and ran downstairs to try to break things up. My friend Steve always said that I'm some kind of diplomat, always trying to create peace, but I had a feeling that tonight's boxing match would prove too much for a 14-year old referee.

The scene was ugly. Ms. O'Reilly was way past drunk.

Her makeup was smeared and her eyes bloodshot. Her boyfriend's face was bleeding from a fresh cut under his eye. The place smelled like somebody poured vodka into a steaming ashtray.

Normally I'm pretty good at creating space between Ms. O'Reilly and whomever she was fighting. These scenes would usually end up with the guy leaving, sometimes on his own, sometimes by police car, but not tonight. Things had gone too far, too fast.

As I walked into the common kitchen area Ms. O'Reilly screamed at me to go away, threatening to kick me out of the house if I didn't go back to my room. She was on some kind of ugly mission tonight and I was in the way. Getting kicked out would have been nothing new because I was kicked out every week or two anyway, and spent half the time sleeping at my friend Steve's house on the other side of town.

"You're drunk and have no clue what you're doing!" I yelled at her. "I have school in seven hours, so either you're leaving or I am!"

She stopped for a second and just stood there, looking at me with bloodshot eyes, panting, like an exhausted boxer between rounds. Her boyfriend was sitting at the table, bleary-eyed, with one hand holding onto an empty glass, and the other wiping his cut eye with his sleeve.

"You have no right talking to me that way," she muttered quietly. "No right at all, you ungrateful brat."

Normally I would try to reason with them like some kind of teenage therapist but not tonight. Exhausted from several days of her funk, and not caring at all what they did to each other, I decided to leave.

I walked into the living room and called Steve to see if I could crash at his place for the night. Although he knew the seriousness of the situation, he laughed anyway and said, "I'll meet you half way, punk." Well-versed in situations like these, Steve could be counted on to be there, day or night.

I ran back upstairs to tell my roommates I was leaving. Even though they were about my age, and were as used to this as I was, they never seemed as concerned as I was about Ms. O'Reilly's drinking and fighting. Unlike me, who seemed to feel and hear everything way too loudly, and felt like I always needed to solve every damn problem in our little universe, they were born with this extraordinary power to block it all out. I know they were upset by her antics, but they always did a better job than me in hiding it.

"I'm outta here, fellas. You might want to keep the door blocked after I leave. I think they're out of booze so they should cool down soon." I grabbed my jacket, Walkman and headphones, and walked downstairs into the hornet's nest. Ms. O'Reilly was sitting on the couch in the living room, smoking and in a daze. There were no words to say so I opened the front door and walked outside into the midnight air.

Once on the street I took a deep breath, let it out slowly, put my headphones on, turned my jacket collar up, and walked into dark suburbia. I looked back to see my upstairs bedroom light on and hoped my roommates would get some sleep soon. I always felt bad about leaving them behind on nights like these, but since I couldn't handle staying there, I had no choice but to leave.

With Grand Master Flash blaring in my headphones, I stepped off the sidewalk and started walking down the middle of the road on the yellow lines, past the busy bar and liquor store across the street from the high school, oblivious to the suburbanites, warm in their cars, honking their horns as they drove around me. Over-tired, frustrated, and with a pounding headache, stupid rules didn't matter.

As a drizzle started coming down I noticed something ahead on the road but couldn't make out what it was. Another car drove by with high beams on and it illuminated the figure about a quarter mile ahead. It was Steve walking towards me, also in the middle of the street! Of course it was. Who else would be walking in the middle of the street besides me?

As I got closer I could hear his boom box echoing off of the sleeping houses. That's just like Steve. He was always on a crusade to share his music, whether people wanted to hear it or not.

Steve discovered rap music a few months ago when his uncle sent him a new record, *Electric Breakdance*, for his birthday. The record had nine songs on it and came with a poster with instructions for how to breakdance. He called me the night he got it and told me to come over right away to listen. Within a few seconds of dropping the needle, we were hooked, big time. The first song on the record, *Jam On It,* by Newcleus, sounded so different than anything we had ever heard before. The beat, the scratching, the funky sounds, all of it was unlike anything on the radio. We played that record over and over again and memorized all the lyrics before midnight. There was even a song called

Magic's Wand by Whodini that gave us a little history lesson on how hip-hop started. By the end of the night we were even trying some breakdancing moves.

Unlike most of the stuff we heard on the radio, the new sounds of hip-hop were exciting, exotic and made us think differently about the world around us. With a radio dial full of bubble gum pop or hard rock, we discovered artists like Grandmaster Flash and the Furious Five, Run-DMC, Kurtis Blow and Lovebug Starsky, who told real stories of ignorance, racism, oppression and never giving up no matter what. Even though we lived over 125 miles away from the South Bronx and Queens, arguably the birthplaces of hip-hop, these songs just made sense to us and we became obsessed with these hip-hop rebels who were trying to change their world with words and art. In the 1970s the kids had punk rock. This was our punk rock of the 1980s. Practically overnight, hip-hop, and everything about it became one of the most important things in our lives. We were all in, with new music, style and attitude. It was like we discovered gold or something.

One of the problems with getting into hip-hop in our town was that record stores in the area didn't sell the music and there wasn't a radio station on the dial that played it, making it really hard to find. A much bigger problem was that our town, which felt like it was stuck in the 1950s, wasn't ready for it. The first time we walked down the street sporting b-boy clothes and a boom box we knew right away that things were never going to be the same. We went from being invisible to being the main attraction for over-grown teenage bullies and jerks, who made it their mission in life to torment or beat us up every chance they had. As hip-hop outcasts we stood out amongst the preppies, jocks and stoners of this Stone Age town and we wouldn't have had it any other way.

As Steve got closer I thought about how we first met less than two years ago. I had just moved in to the Evergreen Foster Home that day and I was sitting on the curb in front of the house drinking a Coke. All of a sudden I heard a car honking its horn as it maneuvered around this kid with long hair and an attitude, who was walking down the middle of the street, giving me a quick nod as he made his way home, like nothing had happened. Like me, Steve had just moved to town and didn't know anybody. In only a few days we became inseparable. I thought about all of our crazy adventures, how we would walk a hundred miles to help each other out of a jam, and how Steve's mother never complained when she woke up to see me sleeping on their couch. She was a saint. Steve and I were like brothers and we saw the world the same way. Even though I had seen him earlier in the day, my eyes teared up as I got closer.

When we finally met in the middle of the road, Steve asked me if I was okay.

"Just the usual," I said, and thanked him for coming with a handshake.

"Let's get the hell out of here," Steve said quietly, putting his arm around my shoulder and offering a fresh cigarette.

We continued walking silently down the middle of the street to Steve's house, while blowing spectacular smoke rings into the crisp midnight air. Nothing needed to be said. Everything was okay.

WHEN BOOM BOXES BOOMED

One thing that adults NEVER understood was that a boom box was much more than a thing that just played music. The portable marvel of sonic boom technology was practically an extension of yourself and your personality. A boom box was a coveted object, respected and indispensable for every kid who lived for music and wanted the world to know it.

And it didn't really matter what kind you had. Yeah, the biggest boom boxes got a lot of attention but every kind of box had unique features, which made them special. Some had speakers that could shake the foundation of the Empire State Building, while others might have cool equalizers, Dolby noise reduction, dual cassette decks, lights, meters or maybe even short-wave radio.

Besides great bass and sound, the most important feature of any respectable box was the ability to record from the radio. Since none of us could afford to buy albums, stealing from the radio was the only way to get new music. The ability to record with no commercials or DJ blabber was a skill to be reckoned with; it took focused coordination, concentration and patience to hold the record and pause buttons down at the same time, while letting go of the pause button at the precise moment when the music started.

Then there was the art and science of making mix tapes. Getting the right songs to fit a certain mood or vibe was a technical skill and the stuff of legends. The best mix tapes were celebrated, re-recorded, and circulated like money.

The music we discovered, worshipped and worked so hard to get made us feel unique in a town, and a world, that expected and rewarded conformity by its young people. By giving us music the boom box helped define our style, our attitudes, and our ideas. But mostly, I think these mighty machines helped this scrappy group of kids find out who we really were, what we stood for, and who we aspired to be, as the music boomed into the stratosphere, woke up the neighborhood, and we made our way into the mad world.

A QUEST FOR MUSIC

"Dude, come on over," Steve said. "My mom's gonna drive us to Connecticut for some new jams." Those were the magic words I needed to hear. It had been weeks since we got any new music. I told him I would be there in 15 minutes, hung up the phone, and ran out the door.

Thirty minutes later Steve, John, Greg and I were in the back seat of a 20-foot long Buick heading south towards southern Connecticut. Steve had his trusty boom box on his lap and John was ripping apart packages of new cassettes.

"Can you drive a further this time?" Steve asked his mother, Susan. "I heard there's a new college station in Hartford that plays the freshest jams after 5pm." Steve's mother said no problem and we cruised onward towards musical hip-hop paradise.

As the old car bombed along the highway we were

giddy with excitement. We couldn't wait to hear what magical sounds the boom box radio would pick up. With the exception of two records all of our music was recorded from radio stations in southern Connecticut or New York City. These road trips were essential to building our music library. We also made a little cash from selling copies of the tapes to desperate high school kids who would pay anything for new music. The cassettes were like gold.

A few miles after downtown Hartford we pulled over at a diner. Susan told us she would grab dinner and read the newspaper so we had at least an hour or so to record. Scanning the FM dial we found what we were looking for and started recording. Sitting in perfect silence we listened to every single beat and word like it was gospel, like it was the first time we had ever heard music. The DJs, with all of their cool slang and knowledge of the artists, were the ministers of funk and we were happy to be in their church.

"I heard that Gary and the freaks tried to run you off the road the other day," Greg said. "What the hell is their problem?"

"I don't know," Steve said. "They're wack."

"You get away?" John asked.

Steve looked up from the boom box. "Of course, man. I ran through a few yards and lost them. They never had a chance."

Greg was referring to a group of older kids in town that made it clear that hip-hop and everything about it, was not welcomed. Gary and his cronies were what we called "druggies" or "freaks" because they smoked pot, drank beer, wore construction boots, only listened to hard rock, and made life miserable for anybody that was different, weak or a threat. For us, the sight of a guy wearing construction boots, jeans, and an AC-DC t-shirt made us very nervous.

We became instant outcasts the first day we walked down the street carrying a boom box. It was serious. It seemed at least once a week we were threatened, jumped or beat-up because of how we looked and the music we loved. It got to the point where we started carrying short wooden clubs in the sleeves our jackets to defend ourselves. Sometimes we carried brass knuckles or a jack knife to keep the freaks at bay. Not that I would know how to use any of them, but at least our primitive weapons helped us feel a little more secure.

The thing that made our crew different than the other kids they pushed around was that we fought back and they didn't like that one bit. The more they threatened us, the more we pushed back. We were proud hip-hop freaks and never, ever backed down.

Greg rolled his eyes. "Pricks, all of them. I don't get it."

Steve tapped the top of the boom box to the beat of the music and looked deep in thought. "I don't know, man. Maybe they just hate everything they don't understand. A lot of people are that way. Hell, they used to burn Elvis records back in the 50s, you know?"

John lit a cigarette and took a long drag. "Just watch the news, man. It's the way of the world since time began, all the stupid-ass racism, wars and stuff." He blew a smoke ring out of the window. "They're just wack, that's all."

Steve tapped the top of the boom box to the beat of a UTFO song. "Well, I hate the bastards, all of them."

I was thinking the same thing. Not that I was comparing our problems with a war, but in a way, it seems like all the madness in the world comes down to people not understanding other people, and not willing to change how they think and what they do. Whatever the reasons, our music, break-dancing, our style and everything that went along with it didn't fit in our little world.

All of a sudden the music stopped. "What the hell?" Steve yelled, hitting the side of the box. "Oh crap, the batteries must have died!"

We were pissed. We drove almost two hours and only recorded for 30 minutes.

"Does anybody have any money?" I asked. "Maybe the diner sells batteries." I already knew the answer. Between the four of us we had a grand total of three bucks.

Steve got out of the car and started pacing. "This blows. Don't tell my mom. I feel bad asking her to drive so far for nothing."

Our hopes for new music were dashed. Steve got back in the car and we just looked at the boom box in silence, as if our staring at it would somehow make it come back to life or something.

Suddenly there was a knock on the car door window. It was Susan. Steve rolled down the window and she handed him a new package of batteries. "I thought you might need these," she said smiling. "You left them on the counter before we left. I'll see you boys in an hour." As always, Susan was always a few steps ahead of us and saved the day.

"How'd she know?" John asked.

"I have no idea. She just always knows," Steve replied, smiling.

Because Susan cared enough to drive us to the edge of the world to find new music, hip-hop would become a huge part of who we were and what kinds of people we would become later in life. Throughout my tumultuous teenage career I would seek out the underdogs as friends and went out of my way to stand up for those that saw the world through a cooler lens. I wished I had thanked her for that.

DOWN BY LAW

As MUCH AS WE ALL were infatuated with rap music and the new hip-hop culture, most of us, whether we admitted it or not, loved some of the other new sounds on the radio. It was for this reason that, although we mostly walked and talked the b-boy ways, our crew wasn't really as "down by law" as Steve would have wanted. The term "down by law," meant that you were somebody who was all in the hip-hop scene, not just a little. You were all in or you were a poser.

With the exception of Prince and Michael Jackson, Steve made it very apparent that any other kind of music wasn't acceptable. I never could understand this because his attitude wasn't much different than Gary and the freaks. The only difference was the style of music. Needless to say, this sometimes caused a little friction in our crew. After all, in many ways, the post-punk and new wave sounds that were coming over from England were just as fresh and cool as some of the rap music coming from New York and Los Angeles.

Because of our "other" musical interests, our style wasn't quite as b-boy as our heroes in the movies *Beat Street* and *Breakin'*, or the b-boys and b-girls we saw when we went to the city. The best way to describe it was kind of a hip-hop and punk look. As much as it would sometimes bug Steve that we didn't always look 100% hip-hop, he reluctantly grew to accept it. Besides, even if we wanted to look the part, none of us could afford it. And, even if we did have the money, there was no place in the area to buy those clothes.

Here are some of the "other" jams that Greg, John and I secretly loved when we heard them on the radio or M-TV during the summer of 1984. In no particular order:

Prince, When Doves Cry: No need to elaborate. Purple Rain, the movie, the sound, the style, the purple rebel's attitude, all added up to just about the coolest thing ever.

Billy Idol, Eyes without a Face: Come on, there was no denying it, the sneer, the sound, the attitude, the post-punk pop sound was perfect. Billy made it okay to dance with yourself. Thanks Billy.

Duran Duran, The Reflex: Probably one of our guiltiest pleasures, but you couldn't help but love their total pop grooves. Plus, the girls loved them too so there is that.

Thompson Twins, Doctor, Doctor: We weren't exactly sure who the twins were in the band but their sound was contagious.

Cyndi Lauper, Time After Time: She could sing like nobody's business, had a style like no other and broke all the conventional rules for pop music.

Wang Chung, Dance Hall Days: One cool dude who made some great jams with cool videos and sophisticated lyrics. Everybody have fun tonight. Everybody Wang Chung tonight. Enough said.

Madonna, Borderline: Like Cyndi Lauper, this woman, who was way too cool for school and rocked the planet big-time. Her style, attitude and perfect pop songs were the stuff of legends.

Tina Turner, What's Love Got to Do With it: Don't trust anybody who doesn't like Tina.

Van Halen, Panama: There was no denying this Los Angeles band's ability to create rock music that actually rocked. They weren't about anything but partying and having a good time. What's not to like about that?

Corey Hart, Sunglasses at Night: Come on, total pop song cheese but the guy made songs that were unforgettable. Plus, who doesn't want to wear their sunglasses at night?

Boy George, It's a Miracle: Like Madonna, Cyndi Lauper and so many others, Boy George broke every rule of what music was supposed to sound AND look like.

Sheila E., The Glamorous Life: Super stylish, a world-class drummer, and a friend of Prince, this lady made some incredible music. Sign me up.

Scandal, The Warrior: We will forever be shooting at the walls of heartache thanks to Patty Smyth and her kick-butt band.

Oh, and anything by the Clash, The Ramones, Tears for Fears, The Smiths, The Cure, David Bowie, Eurhythmics, U2, Sade, and maybe Wham.

Although Steve sometimes accused us of "selling out" to the pop music world, and although we didn't always look the part of hard-core b-boys, I think we were as down by law as anybody because rap music was everything to us. We didn't just listen to it; we loved it, we lived it, and because we were so far away from where the music was, we had to work hard to find it. And besides, it didn't really matter what kind of music it was. The best music was all about young people trying to make sense of the world around them. If that didn't describe us then nothing did.

ALL ABOARD

IT WAS A SPECTACULAR AFTERNOON of doing absolutely nothing. The sun was shining, the birds were singing, and from all appearances, it was an ordinary summer day in the most boring place in America. We had no idea just how un-boring the day would turn out.

We were walking down the street and heading up town to get a pizza. As always, we marched two in the front and two in the back. Steve had his boom box hanging over his shoulder and we were jamming to Greg's latest mix-tape masterpiece as we made our way through town.

"By the way, does anybody have any money?" I asked, realizing that I didn't have a cent on me.

"No worries, I got it covered," John said proudly. He ran ahead of us, took out his wallet and pulled out a big wad of cash.

"YOU have money?" Greg hollered. "What did you do, mug somebody or something?"

Mature years beyond his age, John was our crew's "elder" at the ancient age of 16 years old. Funny, charismatic, sensitive and always willing to put himself into harm's way for his friends, he sometimes felt more like a big brother than a friend.

John's always looked tired because he didn't eat enough and always complained that he didn't sleep. We would often kid around with him by saying he was the only middle-aged teenager we knew. Because he got most of his clothes from a thrift store, and rarely cut his hair, bullies tormented him mercilessly. When provoked, John would transform from a quiet and peaceful soul to a skilled street fighter, never backing down and usually overcoming his opponents. It was because of these fights that he developed the cruel nickname "Spaz."

"The next best thing, punk face," John replied. "I had a good morning at the junk yard."

While we were in school pretending to learn something, John would oftentimes break into the junkyard in town, where he would steal car parts and sell them for much-needed cash. He also prided himself with his innovative technique of cutting holes in the bottom of the car seats to collect lost change that had fallen from passengers' pockets over the years.

"Man, I need to start doing that," Steve said. "Selling mix-tapes isn't cutting it at all."

"I think you actually need guts to do that so I guess you're out of luck then," Greg said, before running ahead. "You better stick to selling mix-tapes, pretty boy!"

"Oh yeah?" Steve yelled. "Why don't you come here and say that!" Steve started running after him and then we all started running down the sidewalk, laughing and having a good time. It was times like these, with these lost boys, that I wished I could have bottled up, and saved for times that weren't so good.

Suddenly John stopped, bent over, put his hands on his knees, and started coughing. And not just a regular kind of cough like when you have a cold. This was a hard cough. We walked over too him.

Steve grabbed him by the arm to keep him from falling over. "Hey are you okay? You okay?"

After another round of hacking he took a deep breath. "I'm alright," he said, taking in another deep breath. "It's no big deal, just a cold, that's all."

Suddenly a car slowed down on the street, and then pulled over ahead of us. We stopped in our tracks.

"Hey faggots!" the driver yelled to us from the open car window. "You know they don't allow homos on this side of town!"

It was Gary, our archenemy, and his stupid cronies, who all looked like they should have graduated from high school years ago. Gary and his barbaric toadies made it their mission in life to make our lives miserable. They hated us because of the music we listened to, how we dressed and how we looked. Breakdancing, boom boxes and rap music didn't make sense to them and they took every opportunity to let us know that. They were older, bigger and usually outnumbered us.

We stood together, giving them a hard look as they got out of the car.

"What the hell do you want, jerk?" Steve said. "There are four of us and only three of you. You're outnumbered."

Although we got pretty used to these scenes, I would usually start shaking and would have to put my hands in my pockets so others wouldn't see. We moved closer together as they approached us.

Gary opened his door and stepped out onto the sidewalk. "We have some unfinished business, b-boy." He gave us a quick look and then focused on Steve. "Just you and me. Your girl friends can watch as I pound your face in." His friends got out of the car and stood behind Gary.

We didn't budge an inch.

"So what's it gonna be Steve?" Gary said, smiling. "You can't run forever. It's a small town."

"You're right, Gary" Steve replied. "We can't run forever but we can run now!"

With that, we started running as fast as we could, off the sidewalk, onto the street, through traffic and towards the end of town. Gary and the Neanderthals jumped back into their car and started heading our way.

"This way," John yelled, panting, as he ran ahead of us. "This way!"

I had no idea what he had in mind but as Gary's car got closer, we ran as fast as we could to keep up.

When we arrived at the train yard Greg looked like he had seen a ghost. "Oh crap," he said. "Looks like they had the same idea." Gary's car was parked next to the tracks. A freight train was going slowly down the tracks.

"What the hell are we going to do?" I yelled. "We'll never outrun his car."

"There's only one thing to do," John said. "Follow me!" John started running towards the train. We ran after him but could barely keep up. I could feel my lungs screaming for air.

"Come on!" John yelled, looking back at us. "Let's do it!" When he got about a foot away from the train he leaped into the air, grabbed onto the rusted ladder, and pulled himself onto the edge. Greg did the same thing a second later, screaming "Holy shit!" as he hoisted himself up into the safety of the open railcar.

"Come on!" I yelled to Steve, who was falling behind because he was carrying the boom box.

As Gary and friends started running towards us I put my hands into the air, jumped as high as I could, and barely caught the ladder. With my feet dangling below,

I locked my arms around the ladder and tried to pull my feet up but they wouldn't budge. I could feel the wind from the steel wheels below. I could hear John yelling something at me but the sound of the train drowned his words out.

"Hold on!" John yelled. "Give me your hand! Give me your hand!"

"Come on!" Greg screamed. "Come on!"

As my grip started to fade, I closed my eyes tight, let go with my right hand and held it as high as I could. After what seemed like an eternity, John and Greg pulled me up by my arms and onto the train.

"Come on!" We all yelled at Steve as he ran alongside. "Jump!"

Steve was falling behind as he tried to keep up with the rolling train. "Go without me!" Steve panted. "I can't!"

"No way!" John yelled.

"Throw the box!" I yelled. "You have to throw it!"

While only a few inches from the train, Steve dropped his box and jumped onto the ladder. As we reached out and pulled him onto the edge his box fell to the ground and smashed onto the tracks.

"Son of a bitch!" Greg yelled into the wind. "That was close!"

"Thanks," Steve said, trying to catch his breath. "That was too close."

As the train lurched forward, we could see our archenemies standing on the tracks with a look of astonishment. One of them picked up Steve's boom box and threw it back down onto the tracks. They were clearly disappointed they didn't catch us.

"Posers!" John yelled.

"Bastards!" Greg followed.

Steve stood up and defiantly raised both of his middle fingers high into the air towards Gary. Gary was yelling something but we couldn't hear him over the sound of the train and the wind in our faces. They couldn't believe we got away. Hell, we couldn't believe we got away.

Sitting on the edge of the open railcar we could see the town getting smaller and smaller behind us. We all started laughing uncontrollably. The best kind of laughing that hurts your gut.

Soon the town, Gary, his stupid friends, and our

problems got smaller and smaller, and then disappeared into the distance.

"Does anybody know where this thing is going?" Greg asked, blowing a perfect smoke ring into the wind.

"Vermont," Steve said. "I think Brattleboro, Vermont."

"Does it matter?" John asked quietly.

A LONG WAY HOME

As the train sped north we sat and watched the world go by. As one small town turned into another one I wondered if there were any kids like us out there. And if there were, were they scared to walk down the street like us? Did they feel like aliens in their own town? I wondered if they thought they were alone like us. I think it's good to see another part of the world every now and then, if only to see things bigger than you.

The train started to slow down as we started to get close to Brattleboro. We didn't want to risk getting caught so our plan was to jump off before it stopped in town.

Steve stood up and surveyed the landscape speeding by us. "On the count of three, jump into the grass!" he yelled into the wind. "Watch out for the rocks!"

We stood on the edge and waited for his command. I wasn't feeling particularly good about this plan but it was better than waiting for the train to stop and getting caught.

"One!" Steve yelled as he held up a finger. I looked down at the rushing ground beneath us. With the screeching of the slowing train, and the wind, we could barely hear him.

"Two!"

I looked at Greg and John and gave them thumbs up. They returned a nervous smile and thumbed me back.

"Three!"

On command we all jumped off of the train (I closed my eyes) and landed with a thud on a grassy area next to the tracks, rolling over and over, until we finally stopped. Greg was laughing his butt off before we finished rolling.

Of everybody in our crew, I knew Greg the longest. He was almost a year younger than me but was the tallest of our gang. His laugh was contagious and his outrageous sarcasm sometimes got him into trouble. We met in the sixth grade and lived in the same apartment complex. His parents were very strict and his father had a bad temper. Although I never asked him about it, I think Greg spent as much time as possible outside to avoid his father's wrath. When his father was mad at him the whole neighborhood heard it. Greg had a nervous kind of energy and was the most daring person I knew; he never turned down a crazy adventure. Even as little kids, we both ran to the beat of a different drummer. We somehow had this idea in our heads that we were different than most kids and that was more than okay. We were so inseparable that most people thought we were brothers.

The train rolled by and we got to our feet. I brushed off the dirt from my pants. "Too bad about your boom box, Steve. I swear I almost cried when I saw it smash to the ground."

Steve smiled. "Yeah, but did you see Gary's face? It was almost worth it."

"Hey, how are we getting back?" Greg asked. "We must be 25 miles from home, maybe more."

"What about your mom?" I asked, referring to Steve's mother. "Could she pick us up?"

"No way," Steve said. "I'd have explain the whole thing and she'd be pissed that we jumped the train."

John walked onto the tracks and looked out at the horizon, from the direction we just came from. "I think there's another train going south sometime tonight." Then he started into another coughing fit. Bending over with his hands on his knees, the coughing seemed like it would never stop. We all just stood there, helplessly watching.

"You okay?" Steve asked, patting him on the back. "That doesn't sound good, man."

John regained his composure and stood up. His face was pasty white. Clearing his throat, he replied, "I'm fine. It's just my asthma or something. It gets bad when I have a cold. I'm supposed to go to the doctor's soon."

"Dude, I've never heard a cough like that," Greg said. "That's not right."

"No worries," John said sternly. "I'm fine. I swear."

Although John was tougher than nails, I could tell that something wasn't right. He never mentioned asthma before. Besides, he was the fastest runner we knew and was never out of breath. Lately he seemed a little out of sorts. It was clear that he was embarrassed by the whole thing and didn't want to talk about it anymore.

Trying to change the subject, I offered, "We could try hitch-hiking."

"There's no way anybody is picking up four guys who look like us around here," Steve said. "We'd be better off walking."

I looked down the tracks towards home. They went on forever. "That could take until midnight. We might as well get started. If there's another train we can try to jump it when it comes around."

We started to march down the tracks, back to the place it seemed we were always trying to leave. Although I wasn't looking forward to the long journey, I felt a quiet peace as we slowly made our way south, with nothing but the sounds of our footsteps and crickets. The sun was still warm, we weren't being chased by anybody, and we were on a mission.

As the shadows and silence grew longer I wondered if maybe we were just too hungry to talk. With the exception of John's occasional hacking, we walked two-by-two in silence. Maybe we were a little scared about walking on the tracks when it got dark. Hell, even if we were scared, nobody would dare mention it. But then I wondered if maybe they all shared the same sinking feeling I had about what happened earlier. Yeah, we managed to get away, but we were still running away. It seemed like we were always running away.

Eventually our stomachs got the best of us and we had to venture into the nearest town to try to find food. Although we were trying to stay away from civilization to avoid Gary, we took a chance that he stayed in town and didn't bother trying to find where the train went. We found a gas station in the middle of nowhere and John treated us all to an assortment of Cokes, Doritos, and coffee cakes. We sat on the curb next to the gas station and enjoyed our feast.

"We should get heading back to the tracks if we want to avoid Gary," Greg said, munching on his last Dorito and throwing the empty bag into a garbage can.

"Yeah, at this pace we won't get back 'til morning." John said.

Steve stood up and started walking away.

"Hey man, where you going?" I said. "You're going the wrong way."

Steve continued walking. We all got up off the curb and started to follow. He stopped at one of those metal cigarette-advertising signs on the curb facing the street.

"Screw Gary," Steve said quietly and looked over at us. "SCREW HIM!" All of a sudden he slugged the metal sign real hard with his fist. The sound echoed in the distance. "SCREW HIM!"

We just stood there, not sure what to do, or what Steve was going to do.

"I'm sick of him." SMASH, SMASH, SMASH, went the sign, as he started battering it with both fists. Greg started to walk towards him but I pulled him back.

"Who the hell is he anyway?" SMASH! SMASH! "Some stupid, spoiled, suburban prick that gets his jollies beating people up who aren't like him." SMASH! SMASH! He started to punch the sign again and stopped. "I'm not running any more." He looked over to us, panting. "No more, man."

Steve was right and we knew it. He said the words we had been feeling for a long time. Although he had a reputation as a tough kid, was a total wise ass to just about everyone, and usually didn't say much to people he didn't know, Steve was one of the smartest people I ever met. But the thing is I often thought that he wasn't comfortable at all with people knowing it, which is why he hid behind his sneer and attitude.

Living with an older sister who was busy with her teenager life, and one of the hardest-working single moms on the planet, Steve needed to figure things out for himself at a young age. He was one of those guys who could take anything apart and put it back together. He just somehow knew how things worked. For Steve, family and friends (and music) meant everything. Nothing mattered more. He was fiercely loyal to his friends and would do anything for them.

"I'm with you," Greg said. "No more."

"Me too," John said, quietly. "Screw him."

"What do you say, Jimmy?" Steve asked. "You in?"

I walked over to Steve and gave him a pat on the back. "You know it, man. No more."

It was only a few weeks ago when Gary and his crew ran me off the road one night while I was riding my bike. Although I tried to get away, they caught me quick. Two guys held me while another one punched me in the face a few times, all while laughing like it was some kind of party or something. My bike was wrecked; I had a black eye and had to walk all the way home.

It was like a cat and mouse game to Gary and his stupid friends. A game. I felt like things were getting rougher every time we met. Although I wasn't sure what our plan was going to be the next time they showed up, I knew that running away wasn't the answer. We finished our Cokes, lit up some smokes, and found our way back to the tracks.

The train never did come. We walked the tracks through the night with only stars to guide us and got back to town around two o'clock in the morning. Although we had only been gone for about twelve hours, it seemed like a week, and I somehow felt a lot older than I was when we left.

"Hey, your boom box should be around here somewhere," John said, breaking the quiet. "Over there."

"I think it's right up there," Steve said as he trotted ahead of us. "Whatever is left of it."

When we caught up with Steve he was sitting on the track with his box in his lap, like a new mother gingerly holding her newborn for the first time. "Hey, it's not too bad, just a few cracks and some scratches," he said proudly. "Kind of makes it look tougher."

GETTING A JOB

IT ALL STARTED ONE DAY when we were walking around town trying to find new sounds for our mix-tapes. When we found a worthy sound, like a phone ringing, a train, or maybe the pitter-patter of rain on the hood of a car, we would plug a microphone into a boom box and record it on tape. Sometimes we would record Saturday morning cartoons or TV shows. We mixed these sounds into music and added new beats and scratching, which made our mix-tapes very cool, unique and highly sought after by kids who were willing to pay two bucks for one of our "super-def" cassettes. We created a library of hundreds of sounds. Nobody made mix-tapes like we did.

One day we found ourselves in the junkyard at the edge of town recording the sound of opening and closing a rusted car door, when we suddenly heard something behind the heap of rusted cars.

"Run for it!" Greg shouted. "To the fence!"

"No way!" John yelled. "It's too far!"

"Screw that, follow me!" Steve shouted. "Over here!"

Before we knew it we were running behind Steve as he sprinted like a madman towards a rusted out old Volkswagen Beetle. We could hear the sound of a truck approaching, probably the junkyard owner.

Steve got there first and threw open the door. "Jump in! And duck!"

At that, we jumped in, crouched down as low as we could, held our breath, and hoped we weren't seen or heard.

Time ticked away slowly. We could hear the truck's engine shut off. Lying on the floor behind the front seats, I could see Greg lying perfectly still on the back seat with his eyes closed tight. Steve and John were laying low in the front seats. It felt like it was 200 degrees in the tiny car. And it stunk something fierce.

Greg opened his eyes and looked down at me. "Are they gone?" he whispered. "I can't hear anything."

"Quiet!" John snapped from the front seat. "I think they're still out there."

As my grandfather always said, I was sweating like Richard Nixon walking through the Mojave Desert in the summer. Sweat was dripping off of me into a pool on the rusted out floor beneath me.

"What's that smell?" Steve whispered. "Are you guys smoking?"

"Not us," Greg whispered back.

"Shit, I think he's right outside!" John whispered. "He's right outside!"

"Don't move; don't breathe." Steve said.

I could smell a cigarette like it was inside the car. I was pretty sure it was a Lucky Strike or Camel; the kind old men always seemed to smoke. The smoke drifted into the car. Then we heard some footsteps. Then nothing.

"Hey you," we heard somebody say. It sounded like an old woman's voice. "What the hell are you all doing in there?"

I was frozen still and ignored the voice.

"Shit!" Steve whispered. "We're screwed."

"Hey, what do you blasted kids want?" she shouted. "Come on out!"

I looked at Greg. Greg looked at me.

"We're busted fellas," John said. "Let's get out and run for it."

We could hear footsteps getting closer.

Steve leaned over from the front seat and looked at John and I. His eyes were bulging. "One…two…three…now!"

On three, Steve and John flung the doors open, rolled out of the car, jumped to their feet, and started running as fast as they could without looking back. The problem was that Greg and I were still in the back seat and couldn't figure out how to push the front seats forward to get out.

"Holy crap!" Greg yelled. "This stupid seat!"

As we fumbled with the seat levers I popped my head up and saw Steve and John booking it fast. They must have been a couple of hundred yards away already. Then I saw the end of a rifle pointing at my face.

"What the hell do you want, you punk kids?" the old woman said. A quick look at her and I could tell that she

41

meant business. She kept the rifle pointed towards me and took a few steps back.

"Umm, nothing." I said quietly. "We were, uh, just looking at the old cars, that's all."

Greg popped his head up from the back seat. "We were just checking out the old cars, I swear." he managed. "Like he said."

"Nice friends you got there," she said, with a half-smile. "They just ran for the hills and never looked back. Come on out." She dropped the rifle to her side and took a long drag of her cigarette.

I finally managed to push the front seat forward and crawled out onto the ground. Greg followed nervously behind me. We kneeled down in the dirt.

"I was, umm, having a little trouble with the seat." I said.

"I can see that. What are your names and where do you live?" she asked. "Stand up already."

"Umm, I'm Billy," I replied nervously. "Billy, umm, Idol. We're, umm, not from around here." I looked over at Greg.

"I'm Lionel." Greg said. "Lionel Richie. Like he said, we're from out of town."

The old woman just stood there, puffing her cigarette and sizing us up. I could tell she didn't believe a damn word we said.

"What do you think, I was born yesterday?" she said, smiling. "What kind of stupid names are those anyway?"

Suddenly Steve and John appeared from behind a pile of scrap metal and started walking over to us with their hands above their heads.

"Get your sorry asses over here," she yelled, pointing the rifle in their direction. "And no funny business either. I might be old but I can shoot a flea off a damn tick from a hundred yards away."

Steve and John stood next to us. Greg and I stood up with our hands in the air.

The old woman lowered the rifle to her side and took another long drag of her cigarette.

"I've been having some problems around here lately with somebody stealing things," she said. "I ain't got time for that bullshit. You wouldn't happen to know anything about that would you?"

We just stood there, motionless, with our hands still in the air. Steve looked over to me. I looked back as if to say I had no idea what to do.

"I'm sorry to hear that lady," Steve said. "But, we were just checking out the cars."

"Yeah, that's what your friends said," she replied, snuffing her cigarette out in the dirt. "I'm not sure I believe you."

"Honestly, that's all we were doing," John spoke up. "Just checking out the cars. We've only been here for a few minutes."

"You can all can put your hands down, except for you," she said, pointing her long wrinkly finger at John. "Everybody step away from the car...except for you."

John looked like he was made of stone. None of us budged.

"I don't believe I've seen any of you around here before but I know I've seen that hat. I've seen you here before, punk, haven't I?"

"I, umm, don't think so," John said nervously. "Must have me mixed up with somebody else."

"No, I don't think so." She stared at John.

We knew she was right. John had coming here once a week for at least year. He told us all about the stuff he stole. He called it a goldmine that nobody cared about. Well, apparently this old woman cared about it. A lot.

"Listen, my husband died last year and I've been stuck with this hellhole ever since. I don't need a snot nose kid like you stealing from me, you got that?"

We just looked at the ground and didn't say a word.

"I've been onto you. You're the one whose been stealing batteries and alternators. I've seen you running outta here wearing that stupid hat."

John stood there frozen like a statue with his hands in the air.

"I already called the cops so you better get your stories straight, you little pricks."

John glanced over to us and then looked back at the old woman.

"I'm, umm, sorry about that," John whispered, looking up at the lady. "It was me."

"John!" Greg said. "No."

John took a step forward.

"John?" she shouted? "You sure it's not Elvis Presley or some other stupid singer's name, like your friends here?"

"No, it's John, and they didn't do anything." he said. "It was just me."

There was silence. She took another cigarette out, lit it up and took a long drag.

"How can I believe you when you don't even know your own damn name?"

"They didn't do anything. I stole the parts."

"What's a kid like you stealing old batteries for anyway? With the way you run you should be on the track team or something."

"I, ah, don't know," he said quietly.

"Speak up, punk. What did you say?"

"I, umm, I needed the money, I guess."

"I need money too but I don't bust into your damn house and steal your stuff, do I?"

"No." John shuffled his feet in the dirt.

"What's that?"

"No, you don't."

"Why do you need the money? Drugs?"

John looked at us and then at the old woman. I would have been scared out of my wits but John wasn't for some reason. He kind of looked relived that he had been caught.

"Things aren't good," he said quietly. "My parents are sick. I have a little sister. I, umm, I sell the parts and give the money to my parents."

The old woman took another long drag. "You can put your hands down," she said.

Suddenly a cop car pulled up with the lights on. We all inched closer together. The officer stepped out of the car and walked over to the old woman.

"Are these the kids you've been having problems with?" he asked, giving us a long look, up and down.

The old woman snuffed out her cigarette on the ground with her shoe. She looked at us, then at the officer, then back at us. We've gotten ourselves into lots of jams before but nothing like this. There was no way out of this. I could see Steve out of the corner of my eye looking around the place for an escape route.

"Thanks for coming so fast, Chet, but I'm afraid I've made a mistake."

"These aren't the kids?" he asked. "That one sure fits the description you gave us last week."

"Nope, I think the guy I'm looking for is a little older. These are just kids passing through."

The officer walked up to John and then glanced our way. I put my shaking hands in my pockets.

"You sure, Dorothy? Didn't you say the guy had a hat just like that?

"Sorry Chet, I don't think he's the guy."

"Okay, if you say so, Dorothy. You gentleman have a good day," he said, giving us the once over again as he got back into his car. "Don't hesitate to call if you need anything, okay?"

"Take care, Chet," Dorothy said. "Please say hello to Susan for me."

"Will do."

I wasn't entirely sure what just happened. One minute we had a rifle pointed at us, the next minute the old woman was letting us go. Or, was she?

"Relax, will ya," she said. "I've seen trouble and you ain't it."

"Sorry about your husband," John said quietly. "I lost my grandfather last year."

"Yeah, things aren't the same around here," she said, scanning the heaps of cars all around us. "I can barely keep up. Where are you from?"

"Umm, I live in town," John replied. "The other side, across the tracks."

"You must be pretty handy around cars, huh?"

"I'm okay."

"Just okay? With the amount of parts you've been taking from me, you must be pretty damn good with cars."

John shoved his hands into his pockets and looked down at his shoes. "I guess so. My dad taught me a lot."

"Well, listen," she smiled. "Rather than you busting in here and me shooting you in the ass, I think I have a better idea."

I looked over at John. I could tell he was nervous. Hell, we all were. Even Steve looked frazzled by the afternoon's events.

"Since you're pretty good with cars and I need the help, why don't you stop by a few times a week?"

John's eyes opened wide. He shuffled his feet in the dirt again.

"Have you ever rebuilt a carburetor before?"

"Umm, maybe, once," John said. "I think so."

"Well, we'll figure something out. I might even give you some dough for your time. What do you say, kid?"

"I would like that. Umm, thanks."

"The name is Dorothy," she smiled. "You boys can call me Dot."

Dot put the rifle over her shoulder and started walking back to her pickup. I felt like I was holding my breath for hours. We all breathed a sigh of relief.

"Holy shit!" Steve said. "What the hell just happened? Did you just get a job?"

"Yeah, that is dope," Greg said. "What a freaking day."

John just stood there with his hands in pockets and sheepishly grinned.

Dot pulled up in her pickup.

"You boys take it easy. John, I'll see you later, okay?"

"I, I will stop by Saturday."

As Dot drove away John stepped forward and waved. I'm not sure, but I swear his eyes were swelling up.

"Hey, let's get outta here," Greg said. "I've had enough of junkyards for a day."

"Word," Steve said. "Let's Jam."

"Anybody up for a Coke?" I asked. "Since John's now an employed dude, he's buying!"

"Yeah, but not for jerks like you!" John yelled. "Last one to the fence is a mouth-breathing poser!"

We all started running as fast as we could towards the fence. As usual, John passed us all like we were standing still, but he suddenly started coughing up a storm and stopped a few yards away from the fence.

THE JACKET

"You guys meet me half-way; I have a cool surprise," Steve said. "It's totally def."

We were all pretty new at figuring out how to dress and look like hard-core b-boys. Without any money and living so far from big cities where they sold real b-boy clothes, we did the best we could in figuring out our style. Out of all of us, Steve definitely led the way and was fearless in making it apparent that he wasn't going to look like everybody else.

After hanging up the phone Steve smirked at himself in his bedroom mirror. New yellow laces on his old Doc Marten boots, black parachute pants with the Velcro pockets, a black Run-DMC t-shirt, a gold-braided rope necklace and a brand new red leather jacket, just like Michael Jackson wore in the awesome "Beat It" music video. Steve was obsessed with the jacket ever since he first saw the video on M-TV and his mother finally broke down and bought it for his birthday.

Grabbing his boom box and keys by the front door, he headed out onto the sweltering afternoon street to walk to my house on the other side of town.

Sweating profusely Steve marched swiftly through the summer heat. He couldn't wait to show off his brand new, prized possession, and nothing, not even 100 degrees, would make him take it off. Blasting Herbie Hancock's "Rockit" into the street, Steve smiled and still couldn't believe what he was wearing. He had THE jacket of all jackets. A few cars honked at him as they leaned out of their windows to get a better look at the sweaty kid marching down the street in the red jacket.

Stopping to change the music, he put the boom box down on the curb and grabbed a cassette out of his pocket. Suddenly a car came out of nowhere, leaned on its horn and swerved towards him from behind. "Michael!" is all he heard as he dove out of the way and landed with a thud on the side of the road. Laying face down in gravel and dirt Steve felt a sharp pain in his chest. Looking up he could see the car stopped on the side of the street a few yards ahead. It was Gary and his friends.

"Hey Michael!" somebody shouted from the car. "You better beat it, like that faggot Jackson says!" Gary and his crew laughed.

Steve didn't move or look up. Still lying on his chest he wondered how many guys were in the car. *The same old bullshit, always outnumbered*, he thought.

Although Steve was about the same age as the rest of our crew he was a little more muscular and could fight like a boss when he needed to. He had a reputation as somebody not to mess with but the fact of the matter was that he never started a fight in his life. Not ever. Not once. His reputation came from his tough attitude and badass demeanor, which helped deter trouble most of the time. But now was not one of those times.

With sweat stinging his eyes Steve strained to pull himself up onto his knees. He could see the source of his chest pain sticking out of his jacket. He winced as he pulled a sharp stick out of his jacket.

The car doors opened and Gary and two of his friends started walking towards him.

"You guys are real tough with three guys against one," Steve said, panting, as he stood up holding the bloody stick. "Want me to call your mammas to see if they can help you because you are about to have a real bad day."

"Oh yeah, what are you going to do about it, MICHAEL?" Gary shouted. "Seems to me that you're all show and no go, as usual. Where are your little breakdancing friends to help you this time?"

Steve thought to himself that he was screwed. His head was aching; he was bleeding into his eye and could feel his blood-soaked shirt sticking to his chest. Normally he carried a short club or a jackknife with him but he was in such a rush when he left that he forgot it. Scanning the ground he spotted a brick next to the curb. They continued walking towards him. A few cars honked their horns as they drove around Gary's parked car.

"Stay back or I'll hurt you seriously," Steve shouted. "I mean it." As they got closer Steve suddenly reached down and grabbed the brick off the ground. Holding it up in the air over his head he told them to get back again. They stopped.

"What are you going to do, throw it at all of us?" one of the guys said, laughing. "You're screwed this time and you know it MICHAEL!"

Steve lowered the brick to his side. "No," he said quietly, wiping the blood and sweat from his eye. "I'm not throwing it at all three of you. I'm throwing it at your piece of shit car's windshield if you don't get the hell out of here." Gary's smile left his face. His friends stopped laughing.

At this point John, Greg and I arrived. We had seen Gary's car parked on the side of the street from several blocks away and figured something was up. We gathered behind Steve and stared the mob down. He was breathing heavy. He turned his head and acknowledged us with a half smile, then stared straight at Gary.

Gary suddenly looked concerned. "You wouldn't do that punk because we'd beat the shit out of you and you know it."

"You're going to beat the shit out of me anyway so I have nothing to lose," Steve replied. "So what's it going to be, bastards?"

There was silence. Steve's hand started to shake because he was gripping the brick so hard. He wiped his eye with his sleeve. Another car honked its horn.

"Fine," Gary said, pointing to Steve. "But the next time you won't be so lucky. You better sleep with one eye open because you're dead meat, man. And your little b-boy friends, too."

Steve just stood there, holding the brick by his side and looking straight into Gary's eyes. Gary muttered something quietly to the others and they turned around to walk back towards the car. "Bye, MICHAEL!" one of them shouted. "Billie Jean is not your lover!" They all started laughing. Steve dropped the brick and let out a deep breath.

As Gary and his friends closed the car doors Steve started walking slowly towards the car and flipped them off with both hands. We could hear the engine start up and an old AC/DC song started blaring from the radio. Gary gunned the accelerator a few times and shouted something to us, but we couldn't hear over the roar of the engine.

As the car peeled out and started to drive away, Greg

suddenly stepped forward, picked up the brick, yelled "Bastards!" and skillfully launched it into the air. Our jaws dropped. As if in slow motion, we could see it spiraling like a football before it crashed through the back windshield of the car.

"Holy crap!" John yelled. "Let's get the hell out of here!"

Running through backyards and side streets we didn't stop until we got to the other side of town. Although John started to cough, he led the way as always and had the form of a marathon runner. We eventually stopped behind a gas station to catch our breath. We did it. It was the first time any of us had ever stood up to our archenemies and got away with it.

"You okay, man?" I said to Steve. "You still bleeding?"

Steve started to peel off his sweat and blood-soaked jacket and looked down his shirt. The entire front of his white t-shirt was red and stuck to his body. "I'll be okay," he replied. "It looks worse than it is."

"I'm glad we got there when we did," Greg said. "That could have been ugly."

Steve put his jacket back on. "Yeah, what took you so damn long?" Steve said, smiling. "That was some kick-ass throw, man. Joe Montana would be proud!"

"That is one def-looking jacket, dude," John said, panting as he tried to catch his breath. "Too bad it's ruined."

Steve started walking away like he was a model on a fashion runway. "Ruined? Hell no! I think it looks tougher!"

From that moment on, when anybody saw that jacket, they knew it was our crew.

STREET ART & GRAFFITI: WE ARE HERE

OFTENTIMES OUR CREATIVITY AND FANTASIES would spill out of our minds and onto an ordinary wall that was in dire need of decoration.

The prospect of spray painting our neon dreams for the general public to see was challenging, mostly because we were so worried about getting caught. The key was preparation. We would draw the picture to scale on paper first, being careful to denote specific colors, shading, etc. And we would always do the deed at night, with flashlights, and at least one designated "lookout" person. And you had to move fast. There was no time for perfection. If we dripped, so be it.

Although there were times when we would simply "tag" a location with nicknames, words or phrases, the real achievements were the glorious colorful productions, which required planning, time and risk. The adrenaline rush of accomplishing those masterpieces in the dark, and the pride we took when seeing them in the daylight, was the coveted prize we sought.

But looking back at this time, there was something else that we were aspiring to do, something much, much greater than simply showcasing our disregard for laws. The real motive, whether we realized it or not at the time, was that we felt like we were invisible and wanted to be noticed. Boys like us, on the fringes of normal, who didn't trust most adults, who were a little too loud and rough around the edges, were not the center of anybody's attention. I know now that what we were really doing was shouting to a busy world that we were alive, right here, right now and had something to say, whether you wanted to hear it or not.

Although those walls have long since been painted over, I'll never forget those spray-painted nights and the teenage graffiti souls who dared to be noticed.

CHAPTER 10

THE TOUGHEST KID IN TOWN

Steve's kitchen table was covered in art supplies, poster-sized paper, spray paint cans and a newspaper. Greg's trusty boom box was playing a new mix-tape with some fresh jams. Coke cans and snacks were everywhere. This is all we needed to make a burner, or as some people would call it, graffiti art. But today was no ordinary burner.

We were on a mission, a mission that mattered. On the front page of the day's newspaper was a picture of a local kid riding his bike, smiling like it was Christmas day and his birthday at the same time. Above the picture was a headline that read "Miracles Happen." The kid was a ten-year-old from town named Jose. He made the front page because he just woke up from a month-long coma after getting hit by a car while riding his bike. Nobody thought he would ever wake up. We thought that was just about the toughest thing we had ever heard. Greg thought the kid deserved to be famous for more than a day so our mission was to create a burner in honor of the toughest kid we knew.

After finishing the scale drawing and figuring out all the colors and shading, we packed up the drawing, spray paint cans, flashlights and other materials into backpacks. Greg grabbed the boom box and we stepped outside into the early evening.

Although we've walked the streets of this town a million times, it always felt different when we were on a mission. Walking by ordinary people who were going through their ordinary days, we felt extraordinary, like we were the lucky winners of a secret prize or something. I think we walked a little faster, and with more confidence, when we were on a mission of some kind or another.

Since it was going to be a long night we decided to stop at Bonducci's Café for some fuel. As always, as soon as we walked in, a few of the customers gave us a double-look. Some gave us a dirty look. We were used to it. We didn't look like everybody else and that was more than okay by us. In fact, if they didn't notice us, we would be disappointed. We sat down at a table next to the window looking out into the street.

"What's up fellas?" the waiter asked, eyeing us over. "What's it gonna be tonight?"

"Coffee and New York cheesecake for everybody," John quickly replied before anybody could say anything. "My treat. Lot's of coffee. We're gonna need it."

We always got the same thing. There was no need to think about it. Once the cheesecake and coffee arrived we got down to the business at hand.

Steve took out the mock-up drawing and unrolled it onto the table. "Don't forget to whistle loud if you see or hear anything."

Greg rolled his eyes. "I know. I know." "We've gone over it a million times."

"Wait, YOU know how to whistle?" John said in his most wiseass way, punching Greg in the shoulder. "I didn't know you were that talented. Wow!"

Greg punched John in the shoulder. "Listen, punk! You're lucky you're bigger than me, otherwise…"

"Otherwise, what?"

"Otherwise I'd throw this damn cake at your ugly ass face!"

At that, Greg picked up a piece of cake and hurled it at John, hitting him right between his eyes. There was silence.

John looked serious and wiped the cake off of his face. "That was real freaking mature, man, real mature. Damn, you got it everywhere."

"I'm sorry dude," Greg replied, handing him a napkin.

Suddenly John's serious face turned into a devilish grin and he hurled his entire cake at Greg, hitting him squarely in the forehead. Pretty soon a totally epic food fight was going down at the noisy table next to the window. Cake was flying everywhere. When we ran out of cake we threw sugar packets. After that, it was salt and pepper. It was freaking glorious.

After our food war it was time to head out to our

destination, which was an empty wall on a building in the center of town. The building was some kind of office so it would be closed. The good news was that the wall was perfect for this burner because it could be seen from the street. That was important since the whole point of this burner was for it to be seen. The bad news was that it would be harder to paint without being seen. It was a chancy situation.

"Well, this is it," Steve said as we stopped in front of the building. "We're a little early. Let's chill for a little while around the corner, until ten o'clock."

We sat on the pavement and leaned against the wall a few yards away, out of view from the street, and waited. It was hard to sit still since we were hopped up on coffee and cheesecake and were amped up to get started. It was like arriving at the starting line of a big race and not being allowed to run.

MIRACLES HAPPEN

G REG OPENED HIS EYES, LOOKED around in a daze, looked at his watch, and yelled, "Holy crap! Wake up! It's three o'clock! In the morning!"

"Oh, crap!" we all yelled. "WE FELL ASLEEP!"

We stood up, groggy, mumbling to ourselves, and started getting ready. We only had a few hours before the streets would get busy with Monday morning traffic so we had no time to waste.

"Let's do this," I said quietly, standing in front of the brick wall that was going to look different in the morning. "For The Kid."

"For the kid!" everybody else yelled, followed by laughing.

"I'll take this side," John said and started walking away from the left side of the building.

Greg started to walk towards the right side. "I'll take the other side."

"Just whistle if you see anybody," Steve yelled at them while sorting out the spray paint cans. "But not too loud!"

"WE KNOW!" Greg and John yelled back at the same. "WE KNOW!"

As Greg and John walked away for lookout duty, I looked at Steve and smiled a kind of nervous smile. He half-smiled back, gave me thumbs up, and threw me a can of black paint to start the outline. "No worries, man," he said. "They have our backs. We'll be done before you know it."

Steve had a cool way of calming people down, which I always envied. Even though I would end up doing everything that everybody else did, I was usually the one who was the most paranoid about getting caught. Without him I probably wouldn't do anything remotely cool. Without me, he would likely end up getting caught doing something stupid. We were a good balance that way.

Even though we had put up a few burners before, we really were making it up as we went along, and weren't exactly sure what we were doing. So many things could go wrong. All it took was one nosey person to call the cops and we would be toast. Because this was the first time we painted in view of a busy street, I was especially nervous. And, since this mural was really big and would take a few hours to do, it increased the odds of getting caught, big time.

Standing in the shadows, John scanned the streets for cars or people. He coughed a few times and was shivering since it was unusually cool for a July night. He lit a cigarette and started blowing smoke rings up into the air towards the streetlight.

On the other side of the building Greg was pacing back and forth, trying to stay warm. With his hood on and hands in his pockets, he surveyed the streets.

"Hey guys, check it out!" Greg yelled and started moonwalking into the middle of the street. "You wish you had these def skills!"

"Shut up, stupid!" Steve yelled back.

"You suck!" John yelled.

Greg turned around and moonwalked back to his original post. "The moves on this kid," he muttered quietly to himself and smiled.

With a flashlight illuminating the bare wall, Steve and I moved quickly. With the exception of the sounds of the spray paint cans, everything was quiet. We had done this so many times that we really didn't need to talk at all. Although John and Greg could paint like bosses too, Steve and I worked on this one together because our drawing and painting styles were similar, which ensured everything looked the same.

As the minutes turned into an hour, John started shivering and was becoming bored. "Hey, hurry up already, will ya?" he yelled. "It's getting cold!"

"Shut up, man!" Greg yelled back. "Light a smoke or something. That will keep you warm!"

Suddenly a car appeared a few blocks away. John quickly ducked into the shadows and stomped his cigarette out. As it got closer he realized it wasn't just any old car.

"Oh crap," he whispered to himself. "Cops!"

John whistled as loud as he could and started running towards us, whistling all the way.

"Son of a bitch!" Greg yelled, as he started running towards us. "Cops!"

"Let's go." Steve said calmly. "We're outta here."

Within a few seconds we threw all of our gear into backpacks and were sprinting towards the safety of a dark alley only a block away.

From where we were standing we could see the cop car pull over and park at the side of the road. The officer rolled down the window and shined a light towards the wall.

"Jesus!" John whispered. "We forgot our flashlight at the wall! We're screwed!"

Holy smokes! He was right. The flashlight was still on and lit up the half-painted wall like a Christmas tree.

The officer stepped out of the car and stood on the sidewalk, just a few yards away from the wall.

"Let's get out of here," I whispered. "We're screwed for sure!"

"Let's go," Greg said. "To the back of the movie theater!"

"Sounds good," Steve said quietly. "Let's go."

John had a look of panic on his face. "But the light. He's gonna know somebody was here."

"It's too late," Steve replied. "Let it go, man."

The officer pointed his flashlight into the alley.

Steve motioned to the theater a few blocks away. "Let's go!" he whispered.

On his command we started running as fast as we could while lugging two backpacks and a boom box. As we started to put some distance between the wall and us, I looked back and saw that John was still standing there. I stopped in my tracks.

"John! Come on! Get out of there!"

We stopped behind a parked bus only a hundred yards or so from where we started.

"What's he doing?" Greg yelled, trying to catch his breath. "Get out of there!

"Get out of there!" we all yelled.

The officer started walking towards the wall.

John looked over to us, held his finger to his lips as if to shush us, then pointed towards the wall with a big smile on his face.

"He'll have to catch me if he can," he yelled in our direction and set off like a cheetah, running towards the wall at full speed with a look of fierce determination on his face.

Greg threw his hands into the air. "What the hell is he doing? He'll never make it!"

"Come on! Come on!" we all yelled.

John ran like the wind as the officer got closer.

"Go!" we all yelled. "Run!"

Just as the officer started to approach the wall, John got there first, swooping up the flashlight with one hand, and made a mad dash back in our direction, slipping out of sight into the dark alley, only seconds before the officer stopped at the wall.

We couldn't believe it! He did it! John was the fastest runner we knew but I had never seen anybody run like that before. He wasn't just a little faster than the rest of us;

he was a lot faster. In fact, if things were different, and he had the chance to play sports, John could have been one of the fastest high school running backs or track stars ever.

Arriving at the wall the officer looked around, pointed his flashlight around the area, and then turned around to walk back to his car.

Before John had a chance to stop, Steve lit into him. "What the hell was that about? You could have been caught!"

"What?" John replied, panting and starting to cough. "What?

Steve glared at him. "If you were caught, we all would have been screwed."

"Yeah, that was pretty damn ballsy but a little too close," I said, patting John on the shoulder. "Holy smokes."

John coughed again. "Just me. I would have been the only one nailed."

Steve was pissed. "What are you talking about? That's bullshit and you know it. All for one and one for all, remember?"

"I knew I could outrun that lard ass," John said with a big smile on his face. "Besides, I have nothing to lose, anyway."

"What's that supposed to mean?" I said. "Nothing to lose."

John looked away. "Nothing, forget it."

Greg patted John on the back. "That was freaking awesome, man. Truly epic."

"Wait, what does that mean?" I insisted. "Nothing to lose? What, are you dying or something?"

John leaned against the wall. "Well, umm, maybe not dying…at least not yet."

"Wait, what the hell did you just say?" Steve said. "What do you mean not yet?"

"What are you talking about, man?" Greg asked. "What the hell?"

John looked down at the ground. "Well, you know how I've had this stupid cough? Well, the doctor thinks it might be something serious. Maybe something bad."

Steve looked white as a ghost. "What the hell? What do you mean, bad?"

John sunk to the ground and put his head down between knees. "He thinks I might have some kind of cancer or something. But he's not sure exactly what kind, or how bad it is, though. It might be okay."

Greg's eyes bugged out and he started pacing back and forth. "That's total bullshit! Bullshit! What the hell do doctors know anyway?"

"Yeah, come on, man." Steve said. "Since when do 16-year-olds get stuff like that?"

John looked up at us. Even under the faint streetlight his face was white as a ghost. "They ran some tests last week and it didn't look good. I've got to go to some kind of specialist next week for more tests."

"Why didn't you say something?" I asked in total disbelief. "I mean, that's heavy, man."

"Because I think it's total bullshit, too" he said. "I think it will turn out to be nothing, that's all."

Suddenly my stomach was in knots and I felt like I needed to throw up. Cancer? I never knew anybody who had cancer. Kids weren't supposed to get that. Not John. I didn't know what to say. Nobody did.

"Look, I'll know more next week, okay?" John offered. "It'll be fine." John paused. "I'll be okay. I promise."

"You're right, man." Steve said. "There's no way that stupid doctor knows what they're talking about. They probably got your tests mixed up or something."

"Yeah," Greg said. "You'll be fine, man. What do doctors know?"

"Hey," John said quietly. "I don't want you guys to worry, okay?"

"I just have one question." I said. "If you might have cancer why the hell are you still smoking, you idiot?"

"Hey, get off my back, punk." John said, smiling. "Before I kick your ass."

Steve extended his hand to John to pull him up from the ground. "Hey, no more secrets, man, okay? This crew sticks together, always, remember?"

John reached for Steve's hand and stood up. "Okay, you're right, no secrets."

I patted John on the back. "You're gonna be fine, okay? You know that, right?"

John half smiled. "Yeah, I know."

After an awkward moment of more silence, Greg picked up a rock and threw it towards the half-painted wall a block away. It suddenly felt cold.

Steve reached out to shake John's hand and smiled.

"You're not pissed?" John said as he shook Steve's hand. "About the cop, I mean. You knew I could outrun that old dude, right?"

"Not at all, you crazy bastard," Steve said, pulling John in for a hug. "Very epic, indeed, Spider J."

"What are we going to do now?" Greg asked reluctantly as he surveyed the alley and street.

I was still processing what John just told us but I was glad that Greg changed the topic.

"What do you mean?" John said. "You're not wussing out now are you?"

"No, man," Greg said. "But the cop. He might be onto us. I think he saw us."

"Yeah, he must know something's up," I added. "He left way too soon. I bet he called for back-up or something."

Steve looked out towards the wall. "It's pretty risky. We still have an hour to go until we're done, at least. And the sun will be up soon."

"I say we get going and come back some other time," I offered. "There's always tomorrow."

"Yeah, what do you say?" Greg said. "Let get outta here. Besides, it's freaking cold."

John shoved his hands in pockets and just kept staring across the way towards the wall.

"John, what do you say?" Steve asked. "John, wanna get outta here or what?"

John didn't reply.

"John?"

John just stared into the distance.

"What do you say, man?" Greg said.

"I say let's finish the damn thing," John said, snapping out of his trance. "We can't wuss out now."

"What?" I said. "We might not have enough time. It'll be daylight soon."

"Come on," John replied. "It just feels like the right thing to do, you know?"

Steve walked over and stood by John. "He's right, I say we do it."

We walked back to the wall, but the high we felt when we arrived hours ago was gone. When we arrived Greg and John went back to their lookout duty on the corners and Steve and I started unpacking the paint. We didn't want to attract any more attention than we already did so we only used light from a nearby streetlight. We painted quickly and in silence with the weight of John's news on our minds.

As we finished the last section, Steve asked me if I wanted to do the honors of signing it. It was our tradition to always sign burners with our crew's nickname, "Rockit", which was short for "Rockit Jam Master Mixing Crew." We got the word "Rockit" spelled with an "i" and not an "e" from the Herbie Hancock song, Rockit, spelled the same way. I proudly signed "Rockit Crew 1984" in bright white paint in the lower-right corner of the wall. No sooner did the paint start drying when the sun started coming up.

After packing up the supplies we walked into the middle of the street to see how it looked in broad daylight. Tired, cold, and jittery from hunger, we marveled at our creation. There it was, almost eight-feet tall, ten-feet wide, and with a dozen colors, a larger than life copy of the picture from yesterday's newspaper. The kid on his bike, smiling and with a huge headline above that said "Miracles Happen." It was always cool to see a picture come to life on a wall but this time felt different, more important, in so many ways.

I pushed John on the shoulder. "I'm glad we didn't leave."

"Yeah," Greg said. "That is one fresh burner, for sure."

"Word," Steve said as he high-fived John. "And not a drip in sight, if I do say so myself."

John just sat there, gawking at our masterpiece, with a big smile on his face.

"Speaking of drip," John said. "You guys have paint smeared all over your faces. I hope that comes off suckers!" He laughed.

"Anybody want a smoke?" Steve asked, pulling out a pack from his jacket.

"Not good for my runner's legs," John said, smiling. "On second thought maybe just one. After all, I have nothing to lose, right?" We all started laughing.

"Stop saying that!" I shouted. "Dude, seriously!"

Steve handed each of us a smoke and we lit them in unison with our Zippo lighters. The scene was perfect. We were in the right place, at the right time, doing exactly what we needed to be doing. There wasn't anyplace I'd rather be.

As I gazed at the wall, I wondered what it was like for other kids who didn't have the same kind of freedom we had. Kids with regular parents, with lots of rules, who played sports, or were in the school band, those sorts of things. It's not that I think our lives were better than theirs, but I sometimes felt a little sorry for them because they might not ever know times like these, with these kinds of friends.

"Nothing beats a good smoke after a serious graffiti bomb," Greg said. "Dig it." He blew a smoke ring into the air. We all laughed.

A few cars started to drive by and honked their horns. One lady rolled her window down and gave us thumbs up. Looking like a bunch of zombies who haven't slept in a few days, with paint smeared on our faces and clothes, two backpacks and a boom box, I suppose we looked like the obvious culprits who defaced public property only minutes ago.

"Hey, I think they're honking at us," Greg said as he started to wave back.

"How freaking cool is that?" Steve said. "That's a first, for sure."

"Oh crap, look!" John shouted as he pointed down the street.

Suddenly a police car appeared in traffic a block away and was heading our way.

Steve patted down his hair and adjusted the collar of his jacket. "Be cool. They didn't see a thing. Was that the cop from last night?"

"I think so," John said nervously. "We can make it outta here if we go now."

"Just be cool." Steve said, as he lit another cigarette. "Chill."

We stayed right where we were and tried to be inconspicuous, which was impossible considering the circumstances. If the morning commuters knew we did it then the cop would surely know. I sat on my hands to keep them from shaking.

The police car slowed down and stopped directly in

front of us. The officer rolled down the window, took off his shades, and gave us a look. It was Chet, the cop from the junkyard. I gulped.

"You boys know anything about that wall?" he asked.

"What wall?" Steve replied innocently.

"That wall, behind you, wise guy."

"Oh, you mean that wall?" Greg glanced at the wall, then back to Chet, and shrugged his shoulders.

The cars were starting to pile up behind the police car. A few cars started honking.

"Yeah, that wall, wiseass," he replied. "That wasn't there yesterday, fellas."

Steve smiled. "Sir, I think that wall was there yesterday." John elbowed Steve in his side. Steve winced.

"We just, umm, stopped here to look at it, ourselves," John offered. "We were wondering the same thing, weren't we fellas?"

"It's pretty awesome, huh?" Steve added.

Chet looked unconvinced. "You wouldn't happen to know who did it, would you?"

"Nope," I replied. "But we'll definitely let you know if we hear something."

Chet nodded and half smiled. "By the way, you shouldn't smoke. Those damn cigarettes can light up an alley at night. You know what I mean?"

We just looked blankly at him. I'm pretty sure our jaws were on the ground.

As he started to drive away he gave us a thumbs up and put his siren on for a few seconds. A few more cars passed by and honked their horns at us.

We were speechless.

THE VERY BIG IDEA

As the summer wore on Gary and his cronies were winning the enduring war of sneak attacks and inflicting pain on our crew. When you're outnumbered, outmuscled, broke, and too young to drive, you need to find other ways of defending yourself against mouth-breathing bullies who live to make you scared and miserable. Although most of our tactics usually worked out in our favor, this particular victory didn't come without a price. The awesome plan that Steve concocted seemed impossibly simple and foolproof.

With the terrible news from John only a few weeks ago, and Steve's recent scrap with Gary and his jerk friends, we needed a major distraction and a way to get justice from a mad world that seemed to be crushing in on us.

"Try to hold him still," Steve said. "I can't handcuff

the damn collar if he doesn't sit still." John, Greg and I did the best we could do to keep Brutus from moving around, but weighing in at over 150 pounds, and towering up to our chests, Brutus the Great Dane had other ideas.

Earlier that day Steve devised a brilliant plan that was intended to scare the crap out of our tormentors. It was genius on multiple levels. Here were the steps:

1. John, Greg and I were all going to bring sleeping bags over to Steve's house and "sleep" on his front lawn, which was less than ten feet away from the busy road. And by "sleep" I mean we were going to pretend to sleep.

2. Steve was going to handcuff himself to Brutus's collar. Brutus was going to lie down next to us, under a blanket, so as not to be seen.

3. While pretending to be asleep we were going to wait for Gary to drive by and harass us. The likelihood of this happening was high since it was Saturday night and they would be driving around looking for trouble anyway.

4. With our eyes half-closed we would wait for them to approach us from the street and, at the last second, Steve would unleash Brutus on them, sending them running away like scared little Cub Scouts after a ghost story bonfire.

Once the collar was secure to Steve's wrist with handcuffs and a short chain, we settled down on the lawn in our sleeping bags. We had all of the essentials to keep us energized for the night ahead. Between the cans of Coke, M&Ms, and Camel cigarettes, we would have no problem staying awake until the action started.

Although we looked ridiculous camped out only a few yards from the street, we didn't care. Seeing the looks on their faces when Brutus the horse dog chased them away would be well worth it.

As the hours passed and the lawn became wet with dew, the excitement began to build. Lying on the ground, under the summer stars, with caffeine, sugar and nicotine coursing through our veins, we were giddy with excitement, trying to keep John's spirits up and talking about the most important stuff in the universe. From the girls we wished we knew, the latest jams, who would marry Madonna first, and how cool Ralph Macchio's crane kick was in the Karate Kid movie, all the bases were covered.

The plan would have been perfect if we didn't fall asleep. But, as the stimulants wore off, and the adrenaline rush waned, our frenzied conversation eventually subsided and we did exactly what we weren't supposed to do. We fell asleep around midnight.

The next thing we heard was total chaos. The quiet of the pre-dawn morning was shattered with the sound of Brutus freaking out. We opened our bleary eyes to see Gary and friends standing on the sidewalk just a few feet away, holding baseball bats, frozen in their tracks, jaws dropped, in total belief at what they were witnessing.

Steve jumped up. "Go Brutus!"

With Steve's permission, Brutus barked a Godzilla bark and bolted straight for our enemies.

"Holy shit!" Steve yelled," I can't get the cuffs off! I can't them off!"

As Brutus lurched forward Steve fell down and started to get dragged along behind him. One of Gary's friends yelled something and they all started running down the sidewalk towards Gary's car, which was parked on the street a few yards away.

Although we were all yelling at Brutus to stop, it was way too late. The horse dog had a mission and he wasn't stopping just because Steve was getting dragged, kicking and screaming, behind him. With Steve yelling at Brutus to heal, and all of us running after them, Gary and friends eventually made it to their car, jumped in and slammed the doors closed.

With Brutus standing in front of the car barking, Steve stood up, brushed himself off and removed the cuffs from Brutus's collar. Once safe in the car, Gary and the morons started taunting Brutus, and revved the engine to scare him (and us) away.

"What's that stupid mutt going to do, bite through the door?" one of them yelled from the back seat. "Nimrods!"

"Get that stupid dog out of the way Steve or you both are going to get run over," Gary said over the roar of the engine. "I'd prefer if it was just you but it's your choice."

With Brutus in front of us, we all just stood there, motionless, defiantly staring them down through the windshield. Porch lights starting coming on around us.

Gary leaned out the window. "Get the hell out of the way!" Gary snarled. "I'm counting to three and you're all toast."

The engine roared.

We didn't budge. Brutus started to calm down as Steve held him by his side.

We didn't anticipate this happening at all. Now what were we supposed to do? This wasn't the plan at all. Brutus was supposed to scare them and they were supposed to drive away. That was it.

As Gary revved the engine and sweat started pouring down my back, I looked around and realized that John wasn't with us. Is he still asleep? Is he okay? As it was his parents would freak out if they knew what he was doing. Nothing needed to happen to John.

"One!" Gary yelled over the engine's roar.

"He doesn't have the guts to do it," Steve whispered to us. "Don't move."

I could feel sweat pouring down my face. I looked around for John.

"Two!" Gary yelled. "You're gonna be dead meat!"

We could hear Gary's friends laughing. A few more porch lights started turning on and some of the neighbors started walking towards us.

"Three!" Gary shrilled and revved the engine even louder. "Now get the hell out of the way!"

Suddenly, out of nowhere, John appeared from behind the car and walked slowly up to Gary's window. Gary looked like he saw a ghost. His friends were silent for once.

"I don't think you're going anywhere any time soon, you asshole," he said calmly. "The cops will pull you over in a second."

Gary looked confused. Hell, we all did. "What the hell are you talking about, Spaz?" The car's engine wailed.

"You're done," John said.

"Time's up pricks," Gary said. "Now beat it!"

John's face was stone and his eyes affixed directly on Gary. I had no idea what tricks John had up his sleeve but knowing him, it was something good.

"The last time I checked it was illegal to drive a car without a license plate," John replied, beaming, as he held the license plate up high over his head.

We were all speechless.

"You son of a bitch, give it back!" Gary yelled. "Or you're seriously dead meat, man."

John just smiled and walked to the front of the car where we were standing, while tucking the plate into his jean jacket.

"I don't think so, Gary," John said. "Not today, jerk."

Gary and his cronies just stared at us through the windshield like we were a circus act or something. As we stood there waiting for the next move, some more neighbors walked up and stood behind us. We must have looked like some motley crew.

"You're going to leave now," John added. "You'll find your license plate somewhere in the high school parking lot this afternoon. If you're lucky."

Our little posse didn't budge. We waited.

After a few seconds of contemplation, Gary turned off the engine, got out of his car and walked up to us. His friends stayed behind in silence. Gary lit a cigarette and sized us all up and down a few times.

"You know…you guys, especially Spaz here, are crazy," he said quietly. "You know that, right?" He took a long drag, looked back at the car, then back to us. I could have sworn he almost smiled.

"Maybe," Steve said.

"Yeah, maybe so," John added. "And the name is John. Not Spaz."

"The plate better be there by noon…John," Gary said, pointing to John and sizing us up and down again.

"Yeah," John said, "Don't worry."

Gary gave us a nod, half-smiled and turned around to walk back to the car.

"By noon," he said, as he climbed into the driver's seat.

We all stepped away from the car and walked back onto the sidewalk.

As Gary pulled out onto the street some of the neighbors started clapping. The old man who lived across the street walked up to John, patted him on the back, and said, "That took some guts, young man." Another neighbor thanked John and said she was sick of seeing the car racing down the street, and that maybe they wouldn't come around here anymore.

"Damn, man," Steve said. "That was literally the coolest thing ever."

"Yeah, that was too cool," I added. "Did you see the look on his face?"

"How'd you get that plate off anyway?" Greg asked. "I mean, who carries a screwdriver with them?"

John just smiled and took the screwdriver out of his back pocket. "Guys who spend a lot of time in junkyards, that's who."

John sat down on the curb. "Hey, we all said we weren't going to take it anymore, right? And besides, I had nothing to lose!"

"Oh, you're gonna get it man! I told you to stop saying that!" Greg slapped him on the shoulder.

As the neighbors started heading back to their houses, we all sat down on the curb with John and started laughing, whooping and hollering up at the summer stars. As usual, our schemes never seemed to work out the way we planned but things turned out okay this time. John had nothing to lose and saved the day.

THE LUCKY ONES

THE NIGHT THAT JOHN GOT revenge on Gary by stealing his license plate was the last time we ever saw him outside of his house or the hospital. Although he never told us directly, his sister Becky told us that he had stage-four bone cancer, which was pretty bad. I guess he didn't want to make us worried so that's why he never told us exactly what he had.

One afternoon Steve got a call from Becky that we should go to the hospital in Boston to see John. Apparently he was moved there from the local hospital to get some special treatment and wasn't doing too good.

Steve's mother drove us out to the city the next day. On the drive out there we tried to distract ourselves with music, beat-boxing competitions, and joking around, but I know that all of us were anxious to see John. Since that night with Brutus, John's coughing got much worse and the medicine he started taking was really taking its toll. Steve's mother tried to lighten the mood by pretending to be interested in the music we were listening to and asking all kinds of funny questions about it.

The night after Steve got the call from John's sister we had the idea of getting John a present. Steve thought maybe we could scrounge all of our money together and buy him a red leather jacket, just like his. Although John loved all kinds of rap and other music, his favorite singer by far was Michael Jackson. When somebody put on an MJ song you could count on John moonwalking down the street, rain or shine, every time. Plus, he borrowed Steve's jacket all the time so we figured that was just about the coolest thing we could get him. Unfortunately the jacket cost over $200, and we were over $100 short, so we left for the hospital without it. We ended up making an MJ mixtape instead, with a custom case that had all our names on it and a picture of John's boom box.

When we arrived at his room John appeared to be sleeping. From the hospital room door he looked frail and older. His parents and sister were sitting at his bedside and talking quietly. They attempted faint smiles when they saw us and motioned for us to come in. The place smelled terrible, like chemicals and detergent, and the fluorescent lights on the ceiling made the room feel cold.

Standing next to John's bed it was all that I could do to not start crying. It seemed like only yesterday when John was running wild and not worrying about stupid cancer, medicine, and doctors. But it was only a few weeks ago.

Greg whispered to John's mother, asking her if he could play some music on his boom box. She smiled and nodded. Greg pressed play on the mix-tape and in a second, John's eyes opened wide and he smiled. He was wearing a black beanie on his head and looked pretty beat up, with dark circles under his eyes and some sort of apparatus on his right arm and shoulder that kept them from moving.

Greg put his hand on John's shoulder. "I thought that might wake you up, punk."

Steve got closer to the bed and tried to smile. "Hey man, you look like hell."

"Oh yeah?" John replied, opening his eyes wide. "You don't look that freaking great yourself. Any run-ins with Gary lately?"

"No, not since that night with Brutus," I said. "We've even seen him drive by a few times but he just keeps going. It's weird."

John closed his eyes and smiled.

"Maybe he's just worried about losing his license plate again," Greg laughed. "That was some move, man. Some move."

"Yeah, it was okay, huh?" John said with his eyes still closed. "Too cool for sure."

John's parents could tell we were speaking in code and moved their chairs away from the bed and back to the wall. His sister looked at me like something was wrong. She stayed by my side and put her hand on John's.

"We figured you might need some def music to pass the time with so we made you this new MJ mix-tape." Greg said, trying to be enthusiastic and handing John the tape.

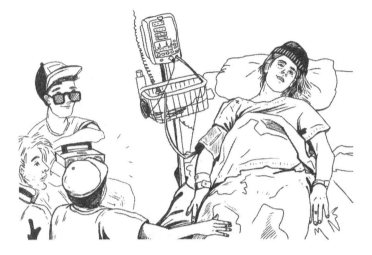

"It even has a picture of your boom box on the cover," I added. "Check it out."

John opened his eyes and took the tape. "Damn, this is cool," he said. "I'll get these nurses moonwalking in no time." He smiled.

There was an awkward silence. What I really wanted to do was bust John out of there and go far away, as if maybe that stupid cancer would disappear little by little, the further we got from the hospital, until it was all gone and John was back to his old self again.

Searching for words, Steve said, "Hey, you remember that time when we were hanging out on the factory roof and we made a bet on who could climb down and touch the street first?

"Yeah...I remember." John looked embarrassed and smiled. His mother and father shook their heads in disbelief. "You bet me that jacket. I almost got killed for that stupid thing. I still say I beat your sorry butt."

"I hate to admit it but you really did whip me. Fair and square, by at least a second."

"Yeah, I know. I just didn't have the nerve to take your precious jacket. It was brand new."

"I always felt a little bad about that, punk. Just a little."

Steve started to take off his jacket and then placed it on John's lap. You could hear a pin drop in the room.

"No way, man," John said. "You don't have to do that. I was just kidding. It was just a stupid bet."

Steve looked serious. "It's yours. A bet's a bet."

"No way, Steve. Besides, I'm going to be stuck in here for a while so who the hell will I impress? The nurses?"

"Hey, you never know. It's yours. Take it or I'll kick your butt in front of your sister." Steve winked at Becky.

"Well, that wouldn't be too hard to do," John said quietly. He smiled, put his hands on the jacket, held it close and closed his eyes.

"You fellas are sweet to stop by," John's mother said, getting up from her chair. "But I think he needs to rest now."

John's eyes opened wide. "What do you say we blow this taco stand and make some noise around here?" John asked. "This place could use some excitement if you know what I mean."

John's father got up from his chair. "John, you shouldn't. The doctor said…"

John sat up. "It's okay, I'll be fine. I promise."

"Okay, just stay in the hallway then. Let me help you."

John pulled the covers off and his father helped him to his feet. Once standing he looked around the room and any sort of pain he was feeling looked like it disappeared.

"What the hell are you posers waiting for?" he said. "But first, my coat!"

After helping him put on the jacket we headed slowly out of the room and started walking up and down the gleaming halls of the hospital. Man, did we stick out like nobody's business. I got the impression, from all of the strange looks we got, that nobody in that place had ever seen kids like us before.

John walked slowly but steady through the halls, saying hello to some of the staff and pointing out this and that along the way. Eventually, the smooth floors became too much of a temptation and all of us, including John, started moonwalking past the nurse's station, with the full intention of annoying them, but instead they ended up cheering us on and asking us to do more!

With John sitting on the floor in charge of the boom box, and the rest of us busting out the best breakdancing we could muster, we ended up becoming the excitement for that night's staff and some patients who stopped by to see what all the commotion about. One thing for sure about our crew was that we really weren't that great in the breaking department. Our only source for learning how to do it was an instructional poster that came with Steve's *Electric Breakdance* album and the movie, *Beat Street*, which we saw once in the theater a few months ago. And that night's audience of about twenty nurses and patients was the biggest and best we ever had and would ever have. As they cheered us on, we got more daring and busted some new moves that we had been practicing. Greg, who was the best dancer in our crew by far, wowed everybody with his windmill and then some girl in a wheelchair started spinning around us all in a circle and rapping to every song! For about fifteen minutes or so, everything was like the way it used to be, the way things should be. Eventually we ran out of moves and the nurses had to get back to work so we all collapsed onto the floor. John was beaming with his MJ jacket on and the boom box on his lap.

"I look pretty damn good in this," John said, turning up his collar. "If I do say so myself."

Greg laughed. "Dude, you're wearing pajamas, white tube socks and old man slippers!"

"Yeah, Michael Jackson never looked so good!" John laughed.

"That's for sure," I said. "We should take a picture and mail it to him. Maybe he can use that look in his next music video or something!"

"Hey Steve, is your neighbor still calling the cops on you for playing your music too loud," John said. "The last time I was there the cops seemed pretty pissed off."

"Yeah, he just doesn't appreciate good music," Steve said. "But I do think the cops are tired of seeing me for sure."

"Well, it doesn't help that you put the damn speakers in the windows facing the street," I said. "What did you think would happen?"

"Hey, it's music education for the neighborhood!" Steve replied indignantly. "I'm just teaching these boring-ass people about what good music is. A DJ for the world, man. They don't call me DJ Tuff Trax for nothing!"

"We're the only ones who call you that, idiot." Greg smirked, punching Steve in the shoulder. "Too bad only a few houses can hear it."

"You just need a bigger voice," John said. "Like, maybe build some big-ass speakers, put them on the roof, and blast them out to the railroad tracks on the other side of town."

"Yeah, that would be freaking def for sure," Steve beamed. "Can you imagine?"

"Wait, I have a better idea. Let's figure out how to build our own radio station or something. Now that would be the baddest! Imagine Gary driving down the road and he hears rap on the radio?" John's eyes lit up.

"Damn, that would be the baddest!" Greg said. "How the hell would we do that?"

"When I get out of here we'll figure it out. I can probably get some cool parts from Dot at the junkyard." John said. "We'll turn this town upside down, man!" John smiled and closed his eyes.

"I'm going to hold you to that, man," Steve said. "A radio station…we'd probably get arrested or something, anyway."

Suddenly John's smile left his face and he turned white as a ghost. He sat there hugging the boom box close to him like it was a blanket.

"Hey, we're coming back in a few days, man," I said. "So, don't take any crap from any of these crazy doctors, okay?"

"You know it," John said quietly. He tried to smile.

"You gonna be okay, man?" Greg asked. "What are the doctors saying?"

John opened his eyes and looked down. "They said I have to get some kind of surgery this weekend." He sighed. "From what I can tell I guess it's a pretty big deal."

This was what I was afraid of hearing. What we were all afraid of hearing. John looked sad and defeated as he leaned against the wall. One of the unluckiest people I had ever known just couldn't get a break.

"You're gonna kick ass," Greg said. "We know it and you know it, okay?" Greg looked down at his feet. I guess he couldn't look John in the eyes. Hell, none of could.

"It's going to take more than a little surgery and chemotherapy to bring Spider J down," John said smiling. "Besides, what would you posers do without me anyway?"

I sat down next to John. "You just get out of here as soon as you can. If you don't, we're gonna bust you outta here."

"Forget that little kid who woke up from a coma. You're the toughest kid in town now," Steve said, pointing to John. "We have to do another burner to tell the world all about it."

"You know it," John said quietly. "You freaking know it."

As we walked John back to his room he started shivering and, as we got closer to the room, he needed to lean on Greg and I to keep going. The excitement of our impromptu breakdancing concert was long gone and replaced with fear, worry and sadness.

I sat in the back seat on the long ride back from the hospital. As I watched all of the cars go whizzing by, with all the busy people going places, I couldn't help but wonder why we all seem to be rushing around all the time. It's like all of us are forever chasing something, always looking to tomorrow for happiness, but maybe today is as good as it gets. I cried a little in the safety of the darkness of the back seat, as the lights of the big city disappeared behind us and we left John alone to fight the biggest fight of his life.

That was the last time we ever saw John. Spider J, the toughest and kindest kid we ever knew, never made it out of surgery that weekend.

The last thing he said to us before we left his room was that he was lucky to know us.

We were the lucky ones.

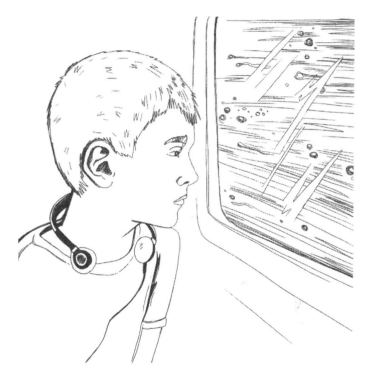

CHAPTER 14

A LETTER

Dear Mrs. and Mr. Vallee,

I can't believe it's been almost two weeks since John passed away. It seems like only yesterday when he was with us. I can't believe he's gone. None of us can. In fact, Steve and I almost called him this morning to see if he wanted to hang out.

I wanted to send a letter to you to say thank you for helping John become the kind of kid that he was. I thought about asking you if I could give a little speech at his memorial service but I was afraid I would mess up the words so I didn't. I know you know how great he was but I wonder if you saw him the way his best friends did. The way I did.

You see John was different from anybody that I ever knew. He was the kind of friend that would NEVER leave you behind. If he cared about you he would literally give you the shirt off of his back. In fact, he actually did that one time when we were swimming in the Connecticut River and my friend Mike got his shirt all ripped up on some rocks. John didn't want him to get in trouble, so he just gave him his shirt. He did stuff like that all the time.

Did you know how funny he was? A few years ago he found this crazy book called *1001 Jokes You Should Never Tell* and would recite the jokes from memory. I swear he memorized all 1001. He had a way of telling these jokes at all the wrong times, which made them even funnier. Man, I miss that laugh of his. We all do.

I know none of us knew you very well, but I could tell you are great parents because of the kind of person John was. He always spoke highly of you and always wanted you to be proud of him. Did you know that?

I suspect you knew that John got into some fights now and then. But I think it's important that you know that he never started a fight. Not ever. In fact, he was one of the gentlest people I ever knew. It wasn't fair how some kids picked on him. I don't think I can ever forgive them.

I remember John telling us once how he got grounded because you found a wad of cash in his room and you thought he stole it. We asked him if he told you where he got it and he said that he didn't. He said he got the cash from selling some car parts from the junk yard but the money was actually for his sister, so she could get a prom dress. He said he didn't tell you because he didn't want you to feel bad because you couldn't afford to get a dress for her. I guess it was bad that he stole the car parts but maybe it was kind of okay since they would have just rusted away eventually and the money was for a good cause?

One thing about John that made him different was that he never complained about anything. A friend of mine, Angelica, was saying just the other day that so many people, who have so much, never seem to be happy but John always seemed to happy. She was right. He always believed that things would get better. I guess that's the definition of hope. I know that times weren't easy for your family, and you didn't have a lot of money, but John didn't talk about that stuff too much. I bet he smiled more than anybody I've ever known.

I could go on and on about what a great kid John was but you already know that. The night after his funeral we all got together and recorded what we called "The 20-Year Tape." On the tape we talked about a lot of stuff but mostly how cool John was and what the future might be like without him. We made copies of the tape for everybody and made a pact to get together in twenty years to listen to it and remember John. The year 2004 seems like forever away but I hope we do that. I can send you a copy if you'd like.

Our crew will never be the same without him. No day will ever be the same. John made everybody and every day better when he was here.

Thank you for reading this letter and for bringing John into this mad world. There are some things, some people, that we don't deserve, and John was one of them. My friend Angelica's mother said the other day that John was too good for this world. I totally agree.

I've enclosed a copy of the only photo I have of him.

This was taken earlier in the summer. We were walking around town one night and John was telling us all about why stars look like they are twinkling but it's really because of dust in the atmosphere or something like that. We spent the whole night talking about space and how mysterious it was. John made us think about things, all kinds of things, in a way school never could.

I miss John so much and will never forget him. He made us better people. Thank you for that.

Sincerely,
Jimmy

CRANK UP YOUR WACK RADIOS

THE DAYS SINCE JOHN'S FUNERAL were a blur. Something seemed off and all of us were in a funk. It felt like something was missing. We were hanging out at Steve's house one night doing something close to nothing, when we decided to hit the street and go for a "walk-about," which was basically walking around looking for something to do. Besides John not being there, there was something else different. It had been a few weeks since Gary and his cronies bothered us. This meant that for the first time in a long time, we weren't worried about getting run off the road or beat up. Or so we thought.

A few blocks from Steve's house was a paper factory. On nights when we were really bored we would hop the fence and climb onto the roof. From there we could see most of the town sprawled out beneath us. Sometimes on hot summer nights we would fall asleep, waking up hours later and walking home under the cloak of early morning stars.

It wasn't too hard getting up to the roof. The hardest part was not getting caught. First we had to crawl under a fence in the back, then over a wall near a loading dock, then run about twenty yards and find a ladder on the back of one of the buildings. Once we were on that roof we could hop from one roof to another with ease.

Tonight we made our way to the roof with silent precision. Once on the top we just sat there in silence and watched the world go by.

"Hey, you guys want to hear something cool?" Greg asked, breaking the silence. He pulled a tape out of his jacket pocket and held it up so we could see.

"What is it?" I asked. "New mix tape?"

"Nope, better."

"Well, go ahead and play it, but not too loud," Steve said, irritated. Steve's mood had been foul since John died. He didn't seem to have any patience for anything anymore. Heck, that was true for the rest of us. Things just didn't make any sense anymore. We seemed adrift without John, without a mission.

"Okay, so check it out," Greg said, putting the tape in the boom box and pressing Play.

The next thing we heard was John's voice, telling one of his stupid jokes, followed by another joke, then the sounds of all of us talking on the night Brutus scared Gary and friends. We all got closer to the boom box and listened intently to every word. "Where did you get this, man?" Steve asked. "This is so cool."

"I started recording stuff after John told us he was sick," Greg replied. "I didn't tell anybody because I wanted it to be real, you know?"

"I get it," Steve said, inching closer to the speaker.

"Wow, that is truly def, man," I said. "This tape is worth a million bucks."

As we listened to our voices piercing the midnight air I was overcome with sadness. Yeah, it was awesome to hear

John's voice again but it just reminded me of something that I was thinking at John's funeral.

"Hey man, pause it. You guys ever hear that old song from Billy Joel called *Only the Good Die Young*?" I asked.

"Yeah, I guess so," Steve said. "So what?"

"I never really knew what it meant until John died."

"What do you mean?" Greg said.

"I mean it always confused me before. You know? Only the good die young? I never understood that."

"Oh man," Steve said. "I never really thought about it. What the hell does it mean, anyway?"

"I think it means that you never really die young if you live, I mean really live, you know?"

"I still don't get it," Greg said. Only the good die young, that's it. He means that only good people die young, that's it. Right?"

"No, it's like he sings about that catholic girl named Virginia and how she's such a goody two shoes, and how she's missing out on a lot of stuff, you know? I think he means that people who don't give a crap about what others think kind of live forever, ya know?"

"Kind of like that Lovebug Starski song," Steve said. "You know, when he says 'Life's too short, we're all gonna die, so go for the gusto reach for the sky?"

"I guess so. I was thinking about that at the funeral, you know? Even though he died young he kind of lived more than most people, you know? The things he did, and the crazy ideas that he had…most people will never know."

"I never thought about that," Greg said. "I hated that stupid old song before, but damn, I never thought about it like that before." Greg leaned back against the chimney and smiled, like he just solved a puzzle or something.

Steve joined Greg, leaned back against the chimney and lit a smoke. "That's heavy, man. Hey, put that tape back on." Greg pressed play again and we listened intently to our voices, to John's laughing, to the sounds of our summer.

"This is almost the end of tape, when we were at the hospital," Greg said.

"Quiet," I said. "Listen."

"Hey, what did he say right there?" Steve said. "Rewind it."

Greg rewound the tape and pressed Play.

> *Wait, I have a better idea. Let's figure out how to build our own radio station or something. Now that would be the baddest. Imagine Gary driving down the road and he hears rap on the radio?*

"Yeah, so what?" I said. "I remember that."

Steve sat up. "I forgot about that…a radio station."

Greg paused the tape. "Yeah, so what."

"No man, you don't get it."

"What do you mean?" I asked.

"I mean, he meant that we should figure out how to make a radio station." Steve rubbed his hands together like he was getting ready to cast a spell or something.

"Wait, for real?" Greg said. "Us? Make a damn radio station? How the hell do you do that, exactly?"

Steve rolled his eyes. "Don't you get it? We could

broadcast hip-hop whenever we want to the whole town, maybe further!"

"Yeah," Greg said. "Make some real noise!"

"I thought he was just kidding around," I said. "Damn, that would be cool."

Steve took a long drag and blew a perfect smoke ring. "It would be the baddest ever."

My mind was racing with so many ideas and questions. "Yeah, but how?"

Steve flicked his smoke off the roof. "Come on, man. Don't be a wuss. I have no idea how to do it but it would be a blast."

I could see Steve's wheels spinning. He stood up and walked over to the edge of the roof.

Greg stood up and walked over to Steve. "What do you say, Jimmy?"

I got up and stood at the edge with them. "You know it."

"Hey all you mouth-breathing zombies out there!" Steve shouted into the dark and laughed. "Crank up your wack radios cuz we got some def jams for ya boring bastards!" As his words echoed off the factory buildings a light drizzle started to fall. "Let's get outta here. We got things to do."

No Way Out

I WAS BEYOND EXCITED AS we climbed our way down from the roof. Even though it was one o'clock in the morning, I had a feeling that sleep wasn't going to happen for a long time. Stepping onto the sidewalk we were already planning and scheming about how the heck we were going to actually do this crazy thing. What would the call letters be? How do you even build a radio station? Where do you get the parts? How much money would it cost? How much power would it need? How far can you hear the music? Is it even legal? So many questions. As we walked through the sleeping neighborhood heading towards Steve's house, overloaded with the prospect of doing something really big, something really cool, it kind of felt like old times again…maybe a little too much like old times.

"Hey," Greg whispered. "Keep walking and don't look behind you, but I think somebody is following us…a car."

"Is it Gary?" I asked. "Doesn't that guy ever sleep?" I could feel the hairs on my arms standing straight up.

Steve glanced behind him. "Must be Gary...the bastard."

"Hey, shut off the box, man," I said. "Quiet." Steve shut it off.

We kept walking like we didn't know we were being followed. The only sounds were our footsteps on the wet road.

"I say we head to the school through those yards," Steve said, pointing to the other side of the street. "They won't find us there."

I glanced behind me and saw the car inching its way up the road without its lights on. "It's a big car. I think it's Gary."

Greg pumped his fist into the air. "I hate that bastard...hate."

"On three, follow me," Steve said. "Boogie your asses off, man. We don't want them to see where we go."

I glanced behind me again. The car stopped and was parked on the side of the street. "Hey, I think it stopped. Maybe it's not Gary."

All of a sudden we were illuminated by high beams, as bright as day, as the car lurched forward and it started barreling its way towards us.

"Three!" Steve yelled.

With the car fast approaching, we ran off the street and into somebody's front yard, then around the house and into the backyard, then over a fence and into somebody else's yard. I couldn't believe how fast Steve could run considering he had his big boom box strapped to his shoulder. A branch from a tree whacked me in the face, almost knocking off my glasses. I could feel the right side of my face stinging as we made our way through a maze of yards and fences.

Pretty soon we ran out of yards and were back onto the street near the school. The neighborhood was dark and quiet. Nothing but sleeping houses. A steady rain started falling. Trying to catch our breath we scanned the neighborhood for Gary's car.

"Damn," Greg said, panting. "You think we lost them?"

Steve spun around and scanned the area. "Maybe. That was close."

"Let's get out of here," I said. "Before they come around again."

Suddenly a car parked in front of one of the houses nearby turned its headlights on, the doors opened all at once, and four big guys started walking towards us.

"Stay cool," Greg said. "We can still get away."

"Yeah, let's see what we're dealing with," Steve said. "They aren't going to chase us on foot." The rain started turning into a downpour.

Steve squinted into the darkness. "Hey, that's not Gary. Who the hell are they?" As they got closer we could see that the biggest guy was holding a bat. They stopped in the middle of the street a few yards away from us. As they got closer I could smell the stench of cheap beer. I didn't recognize any of them and they looked much older than us.

"Hey!" Steve yelled. "What do you want?" We inched closer together.

The big one who was holding the bat turned around to his friends and started laughing, nearly falling over in the process. Then they all started laughing.

"The break-dancer wants to know what we want!" the big guy yelled, as if his friends were a half-mile away instead of right behind him. "What do we want fellas?" They all laughed again.

These guys were different from Gary and his crew. They were driving a new car and weren't wearing the customary work boots and jeans that most of the burnouts around here wore. Instead, they all looked preppy, with their Members Only jackets, like they just stepped out of a JC Penny advertisement or something. They definitely weren't from around here.

"Let's get out of here," Greg whispered. "They're drunk."

"What say you give me that fancy boom box," the big guy said. "Oh, and your wallets too." His friends started laughing like hyenas.

Steve took a deep breath and took a step forward. "I have a better idea," he said, calmly. "What say you go to hell?" Greg and I crossed our arms and gave them our toughest look possible.

Suddenly the big guy's stupid smirk left his face and he lunged at Steve, swinging the bat and totally missing, as Steve jumped out of the way. Then his friends charged us all. One of them pushed me down to the ground so hard that my glasses flung off my face. In a panic I started to crawl around to find them but the same guy kicked me in the stomach with his boot, knocking the breath out of me, and then kicked me in the side.

Everything was suddenly a blur of arms, legs and punches. I couldn't tell who was who and what anybody was saying. Out of the corner of my eye I could see one of the guys on top of Greg, sitting on his back and punching him in the back of his head. I started crawling through the mud, then jumped up and ran towards them, kicked the guy in the side of his face and pulled Greg up off the ground. Before I could catch my breath somebody hit me hard in the back and knocked me to the ground again. I heard Steve yelling something and looked up just in time to see him throw the guy off of me and kick him in the head. "That's all you got!" Steve yelled as he kicked the guy again.

Between the heavy stench of beer and getting the wind knocked out of me, I suddenly felt like I was going to pass out or something. I tried to stand up but fell down. Stumbling, I tried to get up again but as soon as I got to my feet somebody kicked me in the back again and I hit the ground hard, landing on my face first. My heartbeat was the only sound I could make out. Everything started to spin. Then everything went black.

Honk! What was that sound? *Honk!* Where was I? *Honk!* Starting to open my eyes all I could make out were two bright lights fast-approaching on the street. I tried to stand but fell back down, collapsing with a splash in the mud. Everything was chaos. Through the pouring rain I could see Greg out of the corner of my eye, lying on the ground covering his face with his hands, while somebody stood above him, yelling and kicking him in the side. Next to him, two guys were holding Steve's arms back while another one punched him in the stomach. Steve fell to the ground and moaned in pain. The guy started to do some kind of dance, laughing, and then turned around and kicked Steve in his side. Steve lay motionless and let out another moan.

Suddenly a car drove up over the curb, onto the grass and stopped a few feet in front of everybody. Everybody froze. All I could hear was the sound of rain bouncing off the hot hood of the car. All I could see were blinding headlights and smoke pluming from the car's exhaust. I wondered who it was. The cops? Or worse, friends of these guys?

"Hey!" the big guy yelled, squinting through the rain to see who was in the car. "What gives, asshole?" His friends stood next to him, still laughing like idiots.

The car doors opened, three guys stepped out and started walking towards us. Standing in front of the headlights, with plumes of exhaust smoke behind them, all I could see were their silhouettes.

Greg pulled me up off the ground. "You okay?" he whispered. One of his eyes was closed shut. It was all I could do to stand up. My legs were wobbly and I was shaking all over. Steve got up and walked over to us.

The three guys walked towards us. "Oh man," Steve whispered. "It's Gary." I thought about running but I could barely stand up and Steve and Greg were in no better shape. Gary! What the hell did he want? Was he friends with these idiots?

Gary and his two cronies stood next to us. He gave us a hard look, nodded, and then turned his attention to the four thugs.

"Hey, asshole, that was some real fancy dancing," Gary said calmly. "Your mama must be proud."

The big guy took a step forward and paused. "Why don't you beat it; this doesn't concern you, Gary."

"Four stupid-drunk punks on three kids?" Gary said. "Real fair, Joe."

Joe looked back at this friends and then back to Gary. "What's it to you? These little punks had it coming to them."

Gary took another step towards them and folded his arms across his chest. "Why don't you get outta here and go back where you belong before somebody gets hurt?"

"What are you a cop?" Joe snickered. "You're outnumbered tonight, man." His friends laughed a nervous kind of laugh.

Gary glanced at us, gave us a half-smile, and then took another step closer to Joe. "What, are you stupid *and* drunk? I got six guys and you got four."

"What, those twerps?" Joe's friends started to laugh.

Gary walked back over to us and stopped directly in front of Steve. "Hey, you guys need some help with these idiots?" he asked.

Did I get knocked out or something and was dreaming? We all just stood there, not sure what to do or say.

"What do you say, man?" Gary asked.

Steve glanced over to us as if he was asking our permission or something. "Yeah," he said under his breath.

Gary nodded to us and turned his attention back to

Joe. "So there you have it, Joe, six to four. Why don't you get outta here?"

Joe picked up his bat off the ground. "No way, Gary."

"Oh that's how it's gotta be then, huh?" Gary said. "Can you excuse me for a second?" Motioning to his friends to follow, they walked back to Gary's car, opened the doors and got inside.

I looked at Greg and Steve. Greg shrugged. *What the hell was going on?* I thought. *Is he leaving?*

Joe started patting the end of the bat against his hand. "Yeah, that's what I thought. You weren't that good in school but I always thought you had *some* smarts, Gary."

Gary and his friends quickly emerged from the car and walked back to us. Two of them were holding bats while the other one had a golf club. One of Gary's friends offered a bat to Steve. Steve nodded and grabbed it. "I'd say this is as fair as it gets!" Gary shouted. "You're move, Joe!"

It was raining so hard it felt like little spears on my skin. I started to shake uncontrollably and jammed my hands into my pockets. Joe's smirk left his face. He glanced nervously at his cronies, then back to us.

"What's it gonna be, Joe?" Gary said, tapping his bat into hand. "We ain't got all night."

"Okay," Joe said under his breath. "We're going. But they're dead meat the next time we see them…faggot break-dancing punks."

"Oh yeah?" Steve yelled, tapping his bat against his hand. "Give it your best shot, idiot!"

Gary walked slowly over to Joe. Joe's friends looked nervous and took a few steps back. Gary put his hand around him and said something quietly in his ear. Joe nodded, gave us a dirty look and threw the bat on the ground. Gary patted him on the back and then walked back to us. Joe and his crew skulked back to their car. "Let's get outta here," he said. "These little punks aren't worth it."

As the car took off down the street, Gary turned his attention to us. "You guys alright?" he asked. "You okay?"

We looked at each other in disbelief. I didn't know what to say. "We'll be alright," Steve said quietly and handed him the bat. "Umm, thanks."

Gary nodded and half-smiled. "You guys are pretty scrappy but those guys are just plain stupid. It could have been real ugly. Be careful next time."

"Okay, will do," Greg offered. After an awkward pause, Gary and his friends walked back to their car.

I was speechless. Greg and Steve were too. Since when did Gary give a crap about us? *Was this a dream?* Then I felt the pain in my side and realized we were all wide-awake.

Pulling up to the curb and rolling his window down, Gary motioned for us to come to the car. We walked over. Gary lit a cigarette and took a long drag. "I, umm, heard about your friend, John," he said. "He was a good guy... smart."

Gary took another drag. It occurred to me that none of us had ever really talked to Gary before, in a regular sort of way. The only time I had ever heard his voice was when he was snarling at us, and that was usually to our backs because we were running away. He looked out the windshield, then back to us, giving us a long look. "No hard feelings, huh?"

Steve walked closer to Gary's window and put out his hand. "No hard feelings," Steve offered. Gary reached out the window and gave it a firm shake. Greg and I just stood there, speechless. Gary gave us all a look-over one more time, flicked his cigarette out the window and started the car. "See you around fellas," he said and drove off down the street.

Limping through the empty streets, we surely looked like a sorry bunch. It seemed like days since we were hanging out on the factory roof but it was only an hour ago. I guess a lot can change in an hour. The buzz we had from all the talk about the radio station was replaced with disbelief about the fight and Gary, especially Gary. It was like all of a sudden we were in some kind of alternate universe or something. Just when you think you have your little part of the world all figured out, somebody or something comes along and changes it, and you have to figure it all out all over again.

I remember once hearing Joe Strummer from the band *The Clash* say that 'People can change anything they want to. And that means everything in the world.' I guess he was right. In only a few months Gary somehow changed his attitude. If a guy like that could change then I suppose anybody could. But then I wondered about Joe and his posse. Could those idiots ever change? The older I get, the more I think people get stuck being a certain way because things are just easier when you think you have it all figured out. If you don't change then you don't have to do anything different. But, what the heck do I know? I'm soaking wet and fourteen years old.

BLUE EYES

Bing! *What was that?* I turned my pillow over. Bing! *There it is again.* The sound was coming from the window. Rubbing my eyes open, I rolled out of bed and went to the window. Looking outside I could see Greg standing in the yard and holding a rock. I opened the window. "Dude, you're gonna break the window!"

"Get your lazy butt out of bed, man." Greg shouted. "We've got some work to do!" I rubbed my eyes again and looked at the clock. "It's seven in the damn morning!" I shouted, trying not to wake up my roommates. "Hold on, I'm coming down."

It was always like that with our crew. If it weren't Greg throwing a rock at my window at some absurd hour, it would have been me or Steve doing the same thing. What day or time it was never really mattered. Even though it had only been a few hours since I crawled into bed after last night's scuffle with Joe and his mouth-breathing zombies, I was ready for the day. I knew why Greg was so excited. He dreamt about it just like me. Today was a perfect day to try to build a radio station.

"It's about time, man." Greg said as I closed the door behind me and stepped outside. "Let's go wake up Steve's lazy butt."

When we arrived at Steve's house we walked in, greeted his mom, and went straight to his room. We knew he was awake because we could hear the music coming out of his window before we even got to his front steps.

Opening the bedroom door we were assaulted with thumping bass and the sound of scratching. Steve was wearing headphones and standing behind two turntables, scratching one record, while playing another jam at the same time with another record. He had other sounds coming from a dual cassette deck. The setup was what we called his Frankenstein stereo system. We called it Frankenstein because it was really a bunch of different systems all cobbled together. Steve could take apart anything and put it back together again. His stereo was the stuff of legends. Steve acknowledged us with a quick wink and started mixing a *He-Man and the Masters of the Universe* cartoon sound that we recorded off the TV with a Stevie Wonder beat.

Finishing the last scratch, Steve lifted the needle off the record and powered down the stereo. "What took you so long, punks?" he said. "You two look like hell." His hair was a disheveled mess, he was in his underwear and a t-shirt, and was barefoot.

"Did you sleep at all last night?" I asked. "We figured you'd still be out cold?"

"I couldn't sleep much. Too excited, I guess."

"Yeah, me too." Greg said. "I think I got two hours."

There was a knock on the door and Steve's mom walked in. "You boys want some pancakes? You all look like you need some nourishment." She gave us a quick look-over, rolled her eyes and smiled. We probably looked pretty rough after last night so I'm surprised she didn't ask us what happened.

It felt like Greg and I sat at Steve's kitchen table more than our own sometimes and I wouldn't have had it any other way. Things were just different here. Susan talked to us like we weren't just kids. I liked her style. She was a good mother, did all the things a mom should do, but she didn't get into Steve's business too much either. It could be because she was so busy with her two jobs or that she didn't want to know, but whatever the reason, she was all right in my book.

"What's the occasion, boys?" Susan said. "A little early in the morning, even for you guys, isn't it?" She could tell we were up to something.

Scarfing down his second pancake, Steve said, "Not much." Susan wasn't buying it.

"I can't recall you boys at this table so early before. Stay out of trouble, whatever you do today, okay?" She sighed.

"Say, Susan, where would you go to learn everything there is to know about radio stations?" Greg asked. "You know, like how to build one?"

She looked at us over the rim of her glasses with a look of intense curiosity. "I suppose maybe I would start with a book. Remember those?"

Steve smiled. "That's it! Of course, a book!"

She tussled Steve's hair. "Well that was easy. What are you up to?"

Steve quickly went into total fib mode. "Well, err, I was thinking about how expensive it is to call grandma and grandpa in Michigan…My science teacher last year was talking about ham radios and how he uses one to talk to his friends in England. It's pretty cool."

"You're going to build a radio station? In the house?"

Oh no, I thought. Our plan was foiled before we even started.

"Think of the money we would save," Steve offered, like he was selling a used car or something. "No more long distance charges."

Susan sat at the table and gave us a long look. "Well, just be safe and try not to mess the place up. You might want to start with the library. I have to head off to work. Can you boys clean up for me?"

The library! Of course! Why didn't we think of that?

After cleaning up the kitchen, Steve finished getting dressed and we were on the street heading to the library a few blocks away. Besides the one at school, I had not been to a library since I was a little kid. None of us had. They always seemed so stuffy, so quiet, like you had to know some kind of secret code with the Dewey Decimal System, or whatever it was called. I didn't know what to expect.

Our spirits were high as we made our way through the neighborhood. Blasting a new mix-tape on Greg's boom box, and busting out some new breakdancing moves along the way, we were on another mission and nothing else mattered.

Suddenly a car slowed down on the street and the kid sitting in the passenger seat yelled, "Go back where you belong, freaks!" The car kept going and the kid gave us the finger as they continued down the street.

"Yeah, come back here and say that, wimp!" Steve

yelled back. "Come on!" Steve was pissed. *Here we go again*, I thought, *same old crap every day.* "Yeah, that's what I thought!" Greg said, running down the sidewalk and giving the car the finger with both hands. We kept on walking but the joy we felt only a minute before was gone.

It felt like a hundred eyes were on us the second we walked into the library. Dressed to the nines in our best b-boy attire, looking really rough from last night's brawl, and probably looking a little lost, I wasn't surprised at all by the strange looks. But, as John used to say, "It's way better to be bold and noticed than boring and invisible."

Arriving at the front desk, Greg plopped his boom box onto the counter with a loud thud. "Can I help you gentlemen?" the librarian asked, looking us over from head to toe.

"Umm, yeah, do you have any, err, books about radios?" Steve asked. "I mean, about transmitters?"

"Radio transmitters?" she asked. "Books about radio transmitters?"

"Yeah, like how they work and stuff."

"Let me check," she said, still looking us over. "One minute." She left the desk and walked to the other side of the library. We just stood there, awkwardly looking around, trying hard to not look out of place, which was impossible. After a few painstaking minutes she returned.

She dropped a stack of books onto the counter. "You're in luck boys, we have a bunch."

"Umm, perfect," Greg said. "Can we look at them?"

She smiled at us over her glasses. "You know you can borrow them for two weeks, right?"

Greg turned beat red. "Oh yeah, I forgot. Do you need some kind of library card or something?"

"That *is* how it works, young man. Do any of you have one?"

Steve pulled his wallet out of his pocket and placed it on the desk. "How much?"

"For what?"

"For a card."

"Oh, there's no charge, silly; it's free."

"Free?" Steve replied smiling. "We'll take three, then."

The librarian smiled again. "Just a second," she said. "Melanie, can you help these boys?"

"No problem Mrs. Smith," a girl said as she stepped behind the counter. I had seen her before at school. I couldn't help but notice her because she didn't look like most girls in town. Her hair was jet black, she had a pierced nose, wore mostly black and always seemed to be wearing combat boots. I think she was a senior. Definitely not the norm around here. I always thought she oozed cool but never had the nerve to talk to her. And here she was right in front of us! I started sweating.

"You guys need some library cards?" she asked. "You just need to fill these out." She smiled and handed each of us an application.

I wiped my brow and gulped. "Umm, thanks," I said, probably a little too loud. "Thanks a lot." Steve looked at me with raised eyebrows and elbowed me in the side. Greg did the same thing, smiled and gave me a wink.

As we started filling out the applications the girl started thumbing through our books. "You guys building a radio station or something?" she laughed.

"Yeah, umm, something like that," I said, looking up from the application. She had the brightest blue eyes I had ever seen. "Hopefully." Steve elbowed me again.

"That's about the coolest thing I've ever heard," she said, continuing to thumb through the books. "What kind of music?"

"What?" Steve looked up. "What do you mean?"

"If you're making a radio station then you must be playing music, right? What kind?"

Steve looked annoyed. "Umm, we're gonna play hip-hop."

Melanie's eyes opened wide. "Thank God! That's a relief!"

That was not the reaction I expected at all. "What do you mean? You like hip-hop?" I asked in disbelief.

"I'm more into goth and new wave stuff but anything is better than the crap on the radio around here," she said. "I moved here from Cali a year ago and still can't believe how lame the music is here. I've always been interested in hip-hop, though. Love how it is so new." *There she goes again*, I thought, *oozing total coolness*. I never met a girl that looked like her, never mind a girl who loved music the way I did!

Steve looked irritated. "Yeah, well, we're just, umm, playing hip-hop, that's all."

"What do you have in the boom box?" she asked. "Anything good?"

Greg lifted the box off the counter. "Just some stuff we recorded from WBLS FM in New York City and some of our own mixes."

"Okay, that's the second coolest thing I've ever heard," she said with a big grin on her face. "Good luck with the radio station thing. Maybe I'll hear your stuff on the radio sometime."

I wiped my brow again with my sleeve and then handed her our applications. She handed us the books.

"They're due back in two weeks. But if you need them longer, just let me know." Those blue eyes.

Steve and Greg looked uncomfortable and un-thrilled but I didn't care. I kind of didn't want to leave but I knew it might get awkward if we didn't. They started backing away from the front desk. My heart started to race as I just stood there with a blank look on my face. "Hey, what's your number?" I blurted out. *Crap! I blew it!* I thought. "I mean, so I can call you when the station is up and running."

"It's 867-5309," she said, smiling. "Want me to write it down for you?"

"Hah-hah, very funny," I said, embarrassed. "I suppose your name is Jenny too?"

She wrote something down on a piece of paper and handed it to me. "Do you know how many people fall for that one?"

I took the paper from her hand, tucked it safely into my pocket, and turned around to catch up with Steve and Greg who were already at the door, with piles of books in their arms, glaring and waiting for me. Before following them outside I turned around at the door to snatch one more look at Melanie, and to my surprise, she gave me a big wave. I waved back, forgot who I was for a second, and then walked right into the closed door.

CHAPTER 18

LUCKY

WITH A COMBINED TOTAL OF $93 we realized quickly that we couldn't afford to buy all the equipment we needed for the radio station. Greg had an idea to go to the junkyard to see if Dot might have something we could use. John told us that she had this huge garage with all kinds of old stuff. We were in luck! Not only did she have what we needed but she surprised us by saying she was an Army radio operator in the Korean War, which was why she collected all that stuff. Whether it was old transmitters, microphones, or any other radio equipment, she had it. She told us that she was never sure what she was ever going to do with it but she couldn't stand the idea of throwing it away. "It's old, but like me, most of it still works perfectly well," she told us proudly when we walked into the garage.

In my wildest dreams I couldn't picture Dot in an

Army uniform thirty years ago but she pulled out a few pictures from an old photo album to prove it. Although she was thinner, her hair was jet black, and she was sitting in a Jeep, I could tell it was her because her smile, which was kind of crooked and made her look like she was up to something no good. She thumbed through our library books and told us that we should be able to set everything up without a problem. I was never a believer in being lucky but we really did luck out that day. Dot seemed as excited about our radio station as we were. In fact, she gave us her phone number if we had any problems and offered to move all the stuff to Steve's.

Kind of like Gary, Dot reminded me that some people are kind of complicated. What you see isn't always what you get, and they can sometimes surprise you in a good way, if you give them a chance.

We took Dot up on her offer to move all the stuff to Steve's house that afternoon. After unloading the last of the equipment from her pick-up truck, she gave each of us a big hug and told us that she had plenty of work at the junkyard if we were interested in making some extra money. As she drove away all I could think of was that the world needs more people like Dot. And, that I should call Melanie.

DIP SWITCHES AND UNCERTAINTIES

AFTER HELPING GREG DELIVER HIS newspapers the next morning we headed straight to Steve's house. When we arrived, we found Steve on his hands and knees in a mountain and tangle of cords, cables, and equipment in his sun porch. The music was blasting so loud he didn't hear us come in. Holding a smoking soldering iron in one hand while holding an open book in the other, he looked like some kind of mad scientist.

"Yo!" Greg yelled. Steve didn't flinch. "Yo, Steve!"

Steve looked up from the smoke and smiled. "It's about time you got here, freaking posers. Now give me a hand, will ya?"

We spent the next few hours under Steve's supervision. He told us he couldn't sleep at all last night so he got up around midnight and started pouring through all the books. He was the magician; we were the magician's helpers, for sure. He knew exactly what wires went where and which cords went with what equipment.

I had a lot on my mind. The fighting at Evergreen was getting worse and since Ms. O'Reilly had reported me several times for running away, there was a good chance I might have to move to a new place very soon. There was no way I was moving away from my friends, from the only people I trusted. Besides, if I moved then I wouldn't have a place to go if I got kicked out or needed to jam. I didn't know how I would do it but I had to think of something. Last week I walked into the pizza shop a few streets from my house, told them I was sixteen, and applied for a dishwashing job. I wasn't sure if they believed me since I just turned fifteen, but I figured it was worth a shot since I might need cash soon.

I was also starting to worry a little about Steve. Ever since Melanie gave me her phone number at the library he was acting weird. Anytime I mentioned her, he would act like he was mad or something. I couldn't tell if he just didn't like her or worse, that he did like her. Or maybe he didn't like the idea of others hanging around, especially since John died. Needless to say, I wanted to call her but I never did because of the funky vibe I was getting from Steve. The other thing was that he started talking about maybe not going back to school in September, for no other reason than he was bored with it and didn't like it. He hadn't told his mother yet but he seemed to think she would be okay with it as long as he got his GED diploma. He was one of the smartest, maybe THE smartest kid I ever knew, so I couldn't see how dropping out of school would solve any problems. As far as I was concerned, guys like us, who didn't have much to begin with, didn't need to give the world more excuses to look down at us. High school sucked for sure but it was a ticket out of here. My biggest worry was thinking about what kind of trouble Steve might get into without Greg or I around.

Then there was Greg. Like me, Greg thought that he might be moving too. He said his father got laid off from his job a few weeks ago and that they might be moving to another town across the river. Although it would only be a few miles away, when you're too young to drive, and you can't ever get rides anywhere, it might as well be a thousand miles away.

Standing up and lighting a smoke, Greg looked around the mess that was once Steve's sun porch. "Hey, what's the first song we're playing? RUN DMC? Grandmaster Flash? Fat Boys?"

Steve snapped out of his mad scientist trance. "Relax, already thought of that. But we gotta get this thing working first. Jimmy, open up that blue book right there to where I have it tabbed. What does it say about the dip switch setting for our frequency?"

Still distracted by my world of uncertainty, I barely heard what Steve said. "What? What was that?"

"Dude, are you alright?" Steve asked.

"Yeah, umm, what did you say?"

"Grab that blue book over there and open it to the tabbed page. What does it say about the dip switch setting for our frequency?"

I grabbed the book and opened it to the page. "Let's see, hmm, I think you have to know what frequency we are broadcasting from. It's got a grid for all of the numbers. What frequency are we going to use?"

"102.9 sounds available and is all ours." Steve rubbed his hands together like he was about to create magic potion or something.

"Okay, for 102.9 it's on, off, on, on, on, on for the first one."

Steve repeated the numbers back to me as he made the adjustments to the transmitter with a tiny screwdriver. "What's the other one?"

"Off, on, off, off, on, on and off for the second one." Steve made the adjustment.

"So now what?" Greg asked.

Steve sat on the floor beaming, surrounded by all of the equipment, clearly happy about what we created. "I think all we have to do now is adjust the pre-emphasis setting. I think this antique is set for European. We have to switch it to the US setting. Yo, Greg, grab that black book. I've got the page open and underlined the setting. What's it say?"

Greg grabbed the book and opened it up. "It says 75 microseconds, whatever the hell that means."

Steve made the adjustment. "Cool, I think we're freaking all set. All we have to do now is set up the antenna."

STANDING ON A WINDOWSILL TWENTY-FIVE FEET ABOVE THE STREET

"This might be the most stupid thing I've ever done," I gasped. "Give me some more rope you lame punk asses!"

Standing on a windowsill twenty-five feet above the street, with a flimsy rope tied around my waist, a wire tied to my belt loop, a homemade antenna strapped to my back, and a bunch of tools, I was not a happy camper.

A few minutes earlier we were in a heated discussion about which of us would be the sucker to crawl out of the second-floor kitchen window, climb to the top of the roof, and install the antenna. Since we couldn't agree, we decided the best way to choose would be with an honest game of rock-paper-scissors. After losing two out of three, I set aside my fear of serious injury or death and stepped up to do the deed.

Holding on to the edge of the roof, the going was rough and I was sweating bullets. Steve and Greg leaned out of the open kitchen window and pushed my feet up as high as they could. I tried to grasp anything I could hold on the roof above. "Push!" I gasped. "I can't get my feet over the gutter!"

I don't know how we did it but soon I had managed to swing both of my feet onto the slippery, moss-covered slate roof. Parts of the roof were loose or wet, making this whole fiasco more impossible. Even though I had a rope tied to my belt loops, I knew that it would never hold me if I fell. But turning back now wasn't an option. There was no way we were coming this far and giving up. The airwaves were ours to rule.

With Steve and Greg cheering me on from below, inch-by-inch I ascended to the top of the roof. My t-shirt was shredded from the rough slate tiles. As the sweat of my brow stung my eyes, I struggled to pull myself to a standing position by holding onto the brick chimney with all of my might. Just when I thought I could stand, I suddenly slipped, fell flat on my stomach, and started sliding back down, before I somehow grabbed ahold of a wire running across the roof. I tried to hold on but the wire slipped out of my hands and I started sliding back down again, stopping a foot from the edge. "Aaugh!" I yelled.

"You alright?" I could hear Greg yell from below. "You okay?"

My hands were shaking, my stomach and chest were bleeding through my shirt and the sweat was dripping onto the roof like a faucet. I didn't move an inch and tried to catch my breath. "I think so!" I yelled.

"You got this, man!" Steve yelled.

After adjusting all of the equipment hanging off of me, I took a deep breath and started slowly climbing my way back up the roof. I closed my eyes to keep from looking down. The world seemed to disappear as I made my way, inch-by-inch, foot-by-foot, back to the top. I couldn't hear anything other than the sound of my heavy breathing.

After what seemed like forever, I finally got to the top

again, but this time I swung my leg over the other side of the roof so that I was straddling both sides, while holding onto the chimney with one hand.

The world reappeared again. I could hear birds above, the traffic below, and the sound of my heart beating through my chest. "I'm up! I'm up!" I yelled. Steve and Greg were ecstatic below, yelling from the window that I was THE MAN. I was just hoping that I wouldn't fall, or worse, that a pesky neighbor would call the coppers or something.

I pulled myself up into a standing position while setting the backpack and equipment gently down on the roof. "Yo! I'm ready!"

Steve started shouting the step-by-step instructions from below. "Don't attach the antenna until you secure the base, first! Otherwise the whole thing will fall down!"

"I know, I know!" I yelled. After wiping the sweat from my brow, I painstakingly started to install the antenna while trying not to fall off of the roof. First, I needed to duct-tape the barbell base to the side of the chimney. Then I had to attach the antenna to the base with coat hangers and hose clamps. Once in place, I secured the base to the chimney with screws and more hose clamps.

"What's happening?" Steve yelled. "How's it going?"

"It's up! It's up!" I yelled while securing the last hose clamp.

"Okay!" Steve yelled. "Don't move! We're going in to turn it on!"

I lowered myself slowly into a sitting position, leaning my back against the chimney, while straddling both sides of the roof. *After all this, this damn thing better work*, I thought. As the sun started setting, and I waited to hear from Steve or Greg, I thought about John and how much I missed him. If he were here, he would have insisted on being the one to climb up the roof and install the antennae. Man, would he love having a radio station. I thought about how life isn't fair and how he lived every day like it was his last, right up until the end, and how we all should be like that.

As the shadows grew longer, and the sun started dipping behind the horizon, I closed my eyes and my mind suddenly drifted into chaos. What would I do if we moved? Where would I go? Would I get that job at the pizza place? Even if I did, would I make enough money? And what about Greg? If he moved away nothing would ever be the same again. Would Steve really drop out of school? So many questions. When the summer began, everybody and everything made sense. Now, with only a week before the start of the new school year, nothing seemed certain anymore.

"Hey!" I heard from below. "Hey!" I snapped out of it, stood up slowly and walked to the end of the roof facing the street. I looked down and saw Greg holding his boom box up over his head with a big smile on his face. "Steve's going to fire it up in a sec!" he shouted up to me. "We should hear it on my box! Hang on until we know it works!" He proceeded to start moonwalking down the sidewalk, spin on one foot, and moonwalk back. "The moves on this kid," I heard him say to himself. I laughed.

Suddenly I heard music. Loud music! And it was coming from Greg's box! Greg looked down at his box in disbelief, and then up to me, and started jumping up and down. "It works!" he yelled. "It works!"

After a few seconds the music stopped and we heard: "This is Steve, I mean, DJ Tuff Trax, coming at you live from the WRAD studio! This song is dedicated to Spider J, also known as John Vallee! It's a little something called 'You Gotta Believe' from our homeboy, Lovebug Starski, in the Bronx!"

"It works!" I yelled over the rooftops. "It works!" Suddenly my right foot slipped and I came crashing down onto the roof, flat on my face with a thud. After swearing and pulling myself back up, I noticed a piece of paper sitting on the edge of the roof just a few feet away. I reached into my pocket and realized Melanie's note must've fallen out. I got on my knees, crawled to edge and picked it up.

As I watched Greg dancing on the sidewalk from above, with the music echoing off the neighborhood houses, all my worries suddenly disappeared. I thought to myself that there are friends we tolerate, friends we want, and friends that we need. Steve, John, and Greg were the kinds of friends that I needed. We all needed each other and, no matter what happened tomorrow, I would be forever grateful that I ran with the wild ones of the Rockit Crew. Everything was good, right now, at this moment. Everything was just fine. Maybe I didn't know what tomorrow would bring, or the fate of our crew, but as I unfolded Melanie's note and read it for the first time, I knew exactly what I needed to do.

But first I had to figure out how to get down.

Made in the USA
Middletown, DE
01 August 2021

45167217R00094